PASSION FOR MURDER

Tempers flare in this seductive Irish mystery

DAVID PEARSON

THE BOOK FOLKS

Paperback edition published by

The Book Folks

London, 2022

This book is a work of fiction. Names, characters, businesses, organizations, places and events are either the product of the author's imagination or are used fictitiously. Any resemblance to actual persons, living or dead, events or locales is entirely coincidental. The spelling is British English.

ISBN 978-1-913516-29-1

www.thebookfolks.com

PASSION FOR MURDER *is the sixth standalone title in a bestselling series by Irish crime fiction author David Pearson. Details about the other books can be found at the end of this one.*

Chapter One

Dublin City is bounded by two canals. The Royal Canal is on the north side of the city. It used to run as far as Longford on the River Shannon, and in the days before efficient road traffic, the canal carried goods, passengers and livestock from Ireland's longest river to the capital.

The Grand Canal is on the south side of the city, and flows into Grand Canal Harbour which is now a trendy, redeveloped area covered in expensive apartments, bistros, wine bars and fancy eateries.

As you leave the city and travel west out along the Royal Canal, there are many areas where the developers are just waiting to bring in the bulldozers and make their fortunes. These places are characterized by collections of derelict workshops, small commercial enterprises and even houses that have become too damp to be refurbished. Flattening them and starting again is the only option, and of course will deliver the maximum profit for the builders.

But there are still strings of workmen's cottages along the canal too that are in reasonable repair, and it is here that Milo Turner lived on his own with his dog, Shep. It was Milo's habit to take Shep for a walk early every morning. The dog liked to empty himself in the long grass and reeds along the bank of the canal first thing, and Milo, who was retired in any case, was always up early and never in any hurry.

On this particular morning, a damp and overcast Tuesday in late September, Milo fell in with his usual routine. He put on his weatherproof jacket, attached the lead to Shep's collar, and left the comfort of his little house, locking the door securely behind him. Once out along the towpath, he released the dog who went scampering off, sniffing here and there, to do his business. Shep obliged, and then ran off, heading straight for one of the derelict buildings a little further along. Milo wasn't concerned. He knew the dog wouldn't stray far, and Shep was a good deal quicker on his feet than his master, so Milo followed on a little way behind.

When Milo caught up with his pet, Shep was standing still inside an old shed which had no roof, whimpering, and staring at a shape lying on the ground.

"What have you found there, Shep? C'mon, now. Let's go home."

But the dog didn't stir.

Milo decided he'd better have a look. He moved slowly forward, and using a piece of wood that he picked up off the floor from among the general detritus, he prodded the shape a few times. The object was soft and yielding, and as Milo got a bit closer, he could see a mop of dark brown hair protruding from under the rough sacks that covered it. Milo moved in closer, and realised that the object he had been poking was the body of a woman, and she was clearly dead.

Milo recoiled from the body, staggering backwards with the fright, stumbling, and ending up on his backside on the damp floor. He wasn't hurt, but it took him a few moments to gather his thoughts, and start thinking straight again after the shock. He reached into his jacket pocket, took out his old, but serviceable, Nokia push-button phone, and called 999.

* * *

Detective Inspector Aidan Burke was getting ready to leave his bachelor house in Crumlin at just before eight in the morning when his mobile phone started chirping in his jacket pocket. Burke was separated from his wife, Deirdre, and in the usual way of these things, when they parted, Deirdre acquired the spacious family home in fashionable Knocklyon, while Burke was left to find somewhere suitable for himself to live in, with meagre means. He had bought the modest end-of-terrace house in Crumlin from a widow who had reluctantly gone into a home when her husband passed away. The place was in a shabby state, not having seen a paintbrush or a new carpet since the 1960s. But Burke, with some help from his sergeant, Fiona Moore, had done it up quite a bit, and it was now looking much more modern and at least it was clean.

Burke looked at his phone. It was the Garda station in Store Street, where Burke headed up the detective unit, calling.

"No surprise there, then," he said to himself, as he tapped the little green 'accept' icon on the device's screen.

"Burke."

"Good morning, Inspector," said the voice of Danny Reilly, one of the desk sergeants at the station, "we're getting reports of what could be a body found in an old derelict shed up along the Royal Canal, sir. The first responders have asked for a senior officer to attend."

"What could be a body, Danny? You can usually tell – you know, arms, legs, a head, that sort of thing."

Danny was well used to Burke's ironic sense of humour.

"It is a body, sir, and a dead one at that."

"Right. Send me the co-ordinates, and I'll be there in twenty minutes. Get Sergeant Moore out too, and have you called the state pathologist's office?"

"Right, sir, I'll get on it straight away."

* * *

Although the early morning traffic was heavy, Burke arrived at the location in under the predicted twenty minutes. A brightly coloured Garda car was stopped outside the old derelict shed with its lights flashing, and blue-and-white tape had already been erected around the scene which was guarded by a young female officer whom Burke recognised from previous encounters. As Burke approached her, a white Toyota 4x4 pulled up alongside his own car, and Aileen Brophy, the state pathologist disembarked.

"Morning, Aidan. Here, you'd better put this on." Brophy handed Burke a white scene-of-crime suit wrapped in cellophane, and a pair of blue vinyl overshoes.

"I hate these bloody things, Aileen. They never fit properly."

"I know what you mean. And these ones are even worse. The department has a new supplier. They must be Chinese, because the suits are really small. Anyway, they are probably a few cents cheaper than the old ones."

"Terrific!" Burke undid the wrapping and struggled into the white paper suit with a blue line down both the front and the back, much to the amusement of the female Garda standing watch at the entrance to the old place.

Burke and the pathologist, now looking like some kind of zombies, ducked under the plastic tape and went inside. Burke stood back, and allowed Aileen Brophy to go about her grim work. She approached the body, removed the rough hessian covering, and started to examine her specimen.

"Female, very late teens or early twenties by the look of her. Died in situ, judging by the lividity. Some of her clothing has been disturbed, in fact it's torn. She is wearing a cotton blouse and denim jeans – good quality, as far as I can see. Not your usual chain store tat," Brophy said. She looked up at Burke.

"How long has she been here, Doc?"

"The body is cold. That's hardly surprising given the temperature and dampness of this place, but she's still in rigor, so less than thirty-six hours. My guess – and it's only a guess – would be that she died sometime last night, probably before midnight."

"Any idea how she died?" Burke asked.

"I'll need to examine her properly back at the ranch, but I'd say it was definitely not natural causes. I can't see any obvious wounds on her from here, but that doesn't mean anything. If she was, say, strangled, the bruising might not have appeared as yet. It's not consistent. Bruising can appear almost immediately in some cases, and in others it can be days after death. Do you want a look before we move her?"

Burke moved in a bit closer to the dead girl. He got down on his hunkers and looked at the pasty face of the victim.

"She was a nice-looking girl, God help her. Any sign of any identification?"

"That's your job, Aidan, but if you don't mind, I'd like to get her back to the morgue before you start poking around."

"Yes, OK. Will you get to the post-mortem today, do you think?"

"Yes. I'll prioritize it for you. Shall we say two o'clock?"

"Fine. Thanks."

Chapter Two

Burke went back outside the old shed and removed the white suit, struggling a little to get his legs free from the infernal thing. By the time he was restored to normal attire, he spotted Sergeant Fiona Moore getting out of her car and coming towards him.

"Morning, sir. What have we got?"

"Hi, Fiona. A dead woman. Seems she was killed sometime last night. There may be some sexual interference too. Brophy isn't commenting yet. Look, I want this place combed out thoroughly. There's no sign of a handbag or a mobile phone, and she must have had at least those on her. Get a bunch of uniforms up here and arrange a fingertip search of the area. We may have to get divers involved too. If I had just bumped off a girl in this location, I'd probably dump her stuff in the canal."

"Right, boss. Who found her?" Moore said.

"Oh, yes, some old duffer that lives nearby in one of the cottages. The first responders took his details and sent him home. Apparently, he wasn't in great shape after the discovery."

"Do you want to interview him?"

"Dead right, I do. Get his address from the Garda over there, and we'll both go when you've summoned the cavalry," Burke said. He nodded towards the female officer who was still standing guard at the entrance to the premises.

"Right."

* * *

When Moore had finished talking to Danny back at Store Street, Burke and herself walked the short distance along the edge of the canal to Milo Turner's cottage. The house was in reasonable repair. There was some streaking caused by the rain on the outside of the whitewashed building, but the windows, Burke observed, were made of quite new, white PVC, and the glass in them was clean. The front door too was freshly painted in a fashionable mid-grey colour, and the brass door furniture was shining brightly.

Moore pressed the doorbell firmly, and almost at once, a dog could be heard barking inside the little place. A few moments passed. Moore looked at Burke, as if to ask whether she should ring again.

"Give him a minute. He's had a nasty shock."

Several more minutes went by, with the dog inside the house continuing to bark. Eventually, the animal fell silent, and the door opened a little gingerly.

"Mr Turner, my name is Detective Inspector Aidan Burke, and this is my sergeant, Fiona Moore. May we come in, please?" Burke noticed a pronounced whiff of whiskey on the old man's breath.

"Oh, right. Yes, come in. Sorry about Shep. His bark is worse than his bite. But he's locked in the kitchen now."

Turner ushered the two detectives into the small front room of the little house, which, like the rest of the place, was neat and in good general order.

"Sit ye down there. Can I get you anything? A cup of tea, maybe?"

"No thanks, Mr Turner, we're grand. I'm sorry to disturb you. We just wanted to go over the affairs of the morning. Can you tell me what time it was when you found the woman?"

"Let's see now. I left the house at about twenty past seven, as usual, with Shep. So, it would have been about half-past or soon after when the dog went into the old shed, and there she was. God, I got a terrible fright. I fell back on my arse, you know."

"Yes, we were told about that. Did you hurt yourself?" Moore asked.

"Ah, no, I'm grand, but I got a quare fright, I can tell you. Do you know who the lass is?"

"No, we haven't identified her yet. But tell me, is that old place used much by anyone?" Burke said.

"Ah, you get some kids in there from time to time drinking and that, but there's a bad smell in it from some old drain or other, so they don't stay long usually."

"And did you see anything out of the ordinary last night?" Moore said.

"No, not at all. Wasn't I watching telly out the back with the fire lit? It's grand and cosy, and no one bothers me and the dog."

"Who lives in the other houses between here and the old place?" Burke asked.

"You wouldn't believe it now, but that place used to be a factory. When I was a nipper, they made tomato sauce down there. Yes, that's right, tomato sauce of all things. But it closed down a good few years ago, and then the weather took its toll, and the place became derelict."

"But, sorry, Milo, what about the other residents on the street?" Moore said.

"Oh, sorry. Well, there's Mrs O'Brien next door. She's a lovely woman. Keeps herself to herself mind you, but she's grand. Then the next house is empty since old Mr Larkin died last year. I don't know what will become of it.

He had no children, so I don't know what will happen. That's it. Then you're at the factory."

"And did you see or hear anything unusual at all last night, Mr Turner?" Burke said.

"No, not a thing. I was in the back watching telly with Shep until about eleven-thirty. That's when the TV starts all those stupid programmes about American celebritics, so I can't be bothered. But you wouldn't hear anything in any case in that back room. Apart from the TV, it's very quiet."

"OK. Well, that's about it for now, Mr Turner. If you think of anything else that might help us, please let us know," Burke said. He handed the man a business card.

Once outside, Burke said to Moore, "Will you get the uniforms to do a house-to-house all around, and see if there's any CCTV? We need to identify the Jane Doe as soon as possible."

"Righto. What are you going to do?" Moore said.

"I'm going back to the station. I want to get Dónal Lawler started on mispers. If she's a local girl, someone should be getting curious about her by now. I'll see you back in a while."

"OK. See you."

* * *

While Moore waited for the uniformed Gardaí and the divers to arrive, she went for a walk up along the path at the side of the canal. The water moved slowly, and the banks had been invaded by tall grass and weeds, but the water in the canal itself was quite clean, even though there was an amount of rubbish discarded here and there.

"What is it with supermarket trollies?" she said to herself, regarding the two that were visible from her standpoint, sticking up at a jaunty angle covered in green algae and weeds.

Moore had a good eye, and about a hundred meters further along from where the old tomato sauce factory stood, now enveloped in scene-of-crime tape, she came across a muddy patch on the path. She bent down on her hunkers, and examined the ground closely. She saw what she thought might be a track from a motorcycle imprinted in the soft earth, and took out her phone to take several photos of the impression. She walked back to where the forensic team had arrived outside the old building, and directed one of them to the place where she had found the imprint, asking them to photograph it properly and put yellow numbered plastic markers down. Then she went to call on Mrs O'Brien.

* * *

Kathleen O'Brien, by Moore's reckoning, was a woman in her late sixties or early seventies. She was short and stocky, with curly grey hair cut close, and was wearing a floral pinafore over a long, dark-coloured skirt and grey blouse.

"Mrs O'Brien? My name is Detective Sergeant Fiona Moore from Store Street. I was wondering if we could have a chat?"

"Of course, come in. Can I get you a cup of tea, Sergeant?"

"No thanks, I won't keep you long. Have you heard about the incident here last night?" Moore said.

She eased herself in through the narrow door and followed Mrs O'Brien down the equally narrow corridor to the back of the house where a small but well-ordered kitchen smelling of fried rashers and toast was located. When the two women were seated at the somewhat cramped kitchen table that was hinged off the wall, Kathleen O'Brien spoke.

"I heard there was a young one found in the old factory. Was she badly hurt?"

"Yes, I'm afraid she was, Mrs O'Brien. In fact, she was dead when Mr Turner found her this morning."

O'Brien managed to retrieve a tissue from somewhere within her clothing and dabbed at her eyes and nose as she silently wept. Moore allowed her a moment to compose herself.

"I was wondering if you heard or saw anything out of the ordinary here last night between, say, nine o'clock and midnight?"

"Well, I don't know if it was unusual, but there was a bit of a racket going on quite late all right. I'm a light sleeper, and my bedroom is in the front. I usually turn in around ten, read for a bit, and then drop off soon after. Last night I was woken by some noise or other out there, but I didn't get up to see what it was. It's not unusual these days. It used to be so quiet around here, but not recently."

"What sort of noise was there, do you recall?"

"Ah, just general kind of stuff. A bit of shouting, that sort of thing," O'Brien said.

"Did you by any chance hear the sound of a car or a motorbike?"

"Yes, but that was later, after I'd gone back to sleep. It didn't last long, I just heard it revving up and going off down the path."

"Have you any idea what time that was, Mrs O'Brien?" Moore said.

"No, I'm afraid not. But it must have been at least twelve o'clock, I reckon."

"What's the story with the old factory, anyway? Has it been derelict for long?"

"God, it has. Years now. I remember when it was up and running. They made tomato sauce, you know. Gave a good few from round here work too. I even did a bit there myself when my husband was alive. Just for pin money, you understand, and a bit of company," the old woman said.

"Really? When was that exactly?"

"Ah, now let me see. It would have been back in the eighties. It's been closed down a good while. Too much competition from those foreign brands, I suppose."

"And do you see any of the young people that go there to drink or whatever these days?" Moore said.

"I do not. I keep myself to myself. You never know what that lot might get up to if you tried to interfere with them."

"Are they there most nights?"

"No, not usually during the week. Some Fridays and Saturdays, but they don't stay long. Mind you, they can be very loud."

"Is there usually someone on a motorbike with them?"

"No. That's the first time I've heard a motorbike up there."

"May I ask, do you know Milo Turner well?"

"Sure, of course I do. Don't we go to Mass every Sunday up at the church on the Whitworth Road? He's a nice man. Very kind. He sometimes gets my shopping for me if I'm poorly, and I return the favour."

"That's a good arrangement. Right, well if there's nothing else you remember, Mrs O'Brien, we'll leave it at that for now. There will be a few of us around here for the rest of the day, but don't worry yourself, it's all just routine in these cases," Moore said.

"Do you know who the lass was, Sergeant?"

"No, not yet. But we'll get an identity soon, don't worry."

"Do you think we are safe going out after this?"

"Oh, yes, perfectly. This is a very unusual occurrence, Mrs O'Brien. But I'd ask you if you see any more goings-on up at the old factory to call it in to Store Street any time of the day or night. Here's my card with the details."

Fiona Moore left the old lady to her musings, and walked back up to the crime scene where the uniformed Gardaí were getting started on their search among the long grass and reeds at the edge of the canal. She spoke to the Garda standing watch over the entrance to the building.

"Any idea when the divers will be here, Guard?"

"No, Sarge. I heard one of the lads saying that they were on the way though. But it's hardly deep enough for divers. You could wade in there with a decent pair of wellies."

"Rather you than me. No, let's do it properly. I have to get off back to town just now. Will you give me a call if they find anything?"

"Yes, sure, no bother. See you later."

Chapter Three

It was coming up to lunch time when Moore arrived back at Store Street to find Burke in his office looking blankly at his PC's screen.

"Hi. What's the story?" she said.

"There isn't one. Not yet anyway. What did you get, if anything?"

"Same. No ID on the body. The divers are just starting to do a search of the canal. I don't envy them that job, it's full of all sorts. Any word on missing persons?"

"No, not yet at least. But that doesn't surprise me. If she was a student or something, it could be days before anyone realises she's missing, unless of course she was sharing with someone."

"OK. Well, let's hope the PM throws up some good news then. Are you coming across?" Moore said.

"Would you do it for us? I'm not in the humour."

"Yes, OK. Is everything all right, boss?"

"No, not really. But I don't want to go into it now. I'll talk to you later."

"Right, whatever. Would you like me to get you a sandwich? I'm just going to pop over the road," Moore said.

"No, you're OK. I'll go out for half an hour myself in a few minutes. See you later."

"Yes, OK."

Moore hoped that Burke's lunch break wouldn't involve a trip to the local pub and the downing of several pints of Guinness. He had been much better to work with of late since he had reduced his alcohol consumption, and he looked a lot better too. But Moore could see that there was something serious bothering him, and she hoped he wouldn't look for solace in a glass.

* * *

Moore arrived at the mortuary having eaten her sandwich on her own in the office at just before two in the afternoon. Aileen Brophy was all suited up in a green rubber apron with a blue cloth cap over her hair and blue vinyl gloves on her hands. The unfortunate unknown woman was laid out on her back on the brightly polished aluminium gurney with a block supporting her head and a muslin cloth covering her torso.

"Ah, good afternoon, Fiona. I'm just about to start on this one. We have removed her clothing. Ruth Maguire is going over them now."

Brophy turned on the microphone that was suspended over the corpse, and started to describe the young woman as she circled the body, making observations.

"Body of a young woman, possibly in her early twenties, in generally good condition. Height is approximately 170 centimetres, and body weight is 52 kilograms. Some signs of disturbance to her clothing, but no evidence of recent sexual activity and no bruising in the groin area, so she wasn't raped, although some attempt at groping her may have occurred."

Brophy turned her attention to the head and neck of the deceased.

"There's post-mortem bruising starting to appear around the neck area," she said. She moved in closer and took up a magnifying glass to examine the woman's throat carefully.

"There may be some evidence of manual strangulation here, but we will know more in a day or two when the bruising has developed. But there is some petechiae in the eyes, which points to asphyxia. I'll be examining the carotid for damage when we get her opened up. There's no sign of any other head trauma, although there's a lot of grit and dirt in her hair. Probably as a result of where she was killed. Lividity suggests that she died where you found her. The blood has accumulated in her frontal area, consistent with her being left on her stomach after death. Right, let's get inside and see what we've got."

At this, an assistant advanced towards the pathologist with a steel, kidney-shaped dish containing a variety of gruesome instruments. Moore hated this bit, so she went in search of Ruth Maguire, to talk to her about the dead woman's clothing.

"Hi, Ruth. I'm Detective Sergeant Fiona Moore. Dr Brophy tells me you have been examining our Jane Doe's clothes. Anything interesting?"

"Hello, Sergeant. Yes, something a bit strange all right. Have a look at this," Ruth said. She picked up a pair of blue denim jeans and turned them partly inside out to expose the label.

"What am I looking at? And it's Fiona by the way, Ruth."

"Oh, right, thanks. Look here. The manufacturer's label is just as you would expect, but there's another label here too that's in Spanish. It says El Corte Inglés, whatever that means, and then there's some tiny writing in Spanish and some figures."

"El Corte Inglés is a huge Spanish department store. It's a chain. They have shops in all the big towns and cities across the country and on the islands. A bit like Marks and Spencer, but bigger," Moore said.

"Oh, I didn't know. I've never been to Spain," Ruth said.

"Let me take a picture of that label," Moore said. She took out her phone and spent a moment focusing on the tiny fabric label then clicked the camera.

"Anything else, Ruth?"

"Well, her blouse is from Zara. But that could be local. I buy some of my clothes in Zara. It's great value."

"Let me see the label on that too, will you?"

"Yes, sorry, here you go," the woman said. She held out the white cotton blouse and showed Moore the label that was sown into the side seam.

"That's in Spanish too. Do you know if they always use Spanish on their labels, even when the clothes are sold in Ireland?"

"No, I don't, but I'm wearing a shirt I bought there about two months ago in the shop in Henry Street. Would you like me to have a look?" Ruth said.

"Yes, if you don't mind. Do you need to go to the bathroom?"

"Not at all," Ruth said. She opened her lab coat and pulled her shirt up from her trousers, and exposed the label on her top.

"Have a look. I can't see it from here," she said, giggling a little.

"OK, let's see. No. It's all English. Size, style number, washing instructions and so on. No Spanish anywhere."

"I guess that means that she bought the clothes in Spain then," Ruth said.

"Yes, probably. But Spain is a big place. Here, let me get a picture of that label too, and I'll get someone to contact the retailer to see if we can narrow it down at all."

Ruth obliged, and Moore added the Zara label to the photo library on her phone.

"What about the rest of her stuff?" Moore said.

"Well, she had Calvin Klein pants. The labels on those are in English. Size 10. Her bra is Victoria's Secret. Plain white, lacy, and 32B."

"OK, thanks, Ruth. Anything in the pockets?"

"Oh, yes, I nearly forgot to mention it. The only thing we found was a small slip of paper with some numbers on it. Hang on, I'll get it."

Ruth went to her desk and returned with a small clear plastic bag with a piece of white paper inside. Written in blue biro across the page there was a series of numbers – 34694702191375. The numbers were formed in a European style, with a bar across the sevens and a distinct loop at the base of the two.

"Any prints anywhere?" Moore said.

"No, 'fraid not. One last thing. She had a small gold-coloured anklet on her left leg. I think it might be real gold, with some beads set into it. I'll get it for you."

Ruth went to her desk and appeared back with another small plastic bag. Moore could see the little piece of jewellery inside. It was very delicate, like filigree, and set into it at intervals were coloured stones in red, blue, purple and green.

"Is there a mark on it at all?" Moore said.

"Yes, in tiny writing near the clasp, it says 975 as far as I can make out. It's very hard to see."

"That's almost pure gold then. What does it weigh?"

"I haven't weighed it. Hang on, I'll get our scales."

Ruth brought out a small battery-operated scale and emptied the anklet out onto it.

"Just short of 8 grams," she said.

"OK, so let's say half the weight is in the stones, so it's worth about €200 then," Moore said.

"Wow! Not bad, eh?"

"Yes. It could even be more if any of those stones are genuine gemstones. I'll have it examined by a jeweller when you've finished with it. Make sure there are no flakes of skin caught up in it anywhere, and if there are, have them analysed for DNA, OK?"

"Yes, of course, Fiona. I'll let you know."

"Thanks. I'd better get back to Dr Brophy and see if she's found anything."

Back at the gurney, the unfortunate girl had been opened up, and the major organs removed to be weighed and preserved. Moore approached, trying to suppress the nauseousness that sometimes threatened to overcome her at this point in proceedings.

"Well, Doctor, anything unusual?" Moore said.

"Not so far. She was in very good health by the looks of things, although I'll have to get her blood analysed for toxins. That will tell us if she was taking any drugs or whatever. But, no, I'd say she was just a normal healthy woman before this happened to her. Was Ruth any help?" Brophy said.

"Yes, she was. There is some evidence that she may be Spanish, or at least have been to Spain quite recently. But that's just circumstantial for now. Is there any sign of sexual interference?" Moore said.

"It looks as if she had sex within the last forty-eight hours, but I don't think she was raped or anything."

"Will you be able to get swabs and a DNA sample of the donor?"

"Maybe. There may be some traces of semen, but I'll know later," Brophy said.

"Right, well I think I'll be off now. Send over the tox report when you get it. Thanks."

"Of course. Catch you later," Brophy said.

* * *

Later that day, Aidan Burke assembled his small team of detectives in his office. Dónal Lawler and Amy Sutton, who were both Detective Gardaí, joined Moore and himself to review what they knew so far about the dead girl

"So, what have we got? Fiona?" Burke said.

Moore relayed what she had learnt from the post-mortem, including the information about the piece of jewellery that the woman had been wearing.

"Well then. Would it be too much of a stretch to assume that the deceased is Spanish?" Burke said in his usual ironic tone.

"Looks like it, boss, but I'm not sure that helps much," Moore said.

"Why don't we get an image produced and circulate it to the media? We might be able to put up some small posters in the area that she was found too," Lawler said.

"Good idea, Dónal. Will you look after that for us?" Burke said.

"Yes, of course."

"I wonder if she might have been here to learn English, sir?" Amy Sutton said a little shyly. Amy was the junior member of the team and hadn't really found her voice yet among the more seasoned detectives.

"It's quite possible, I suppose. Why don't you do a ring-around of the English schools here in the city and see if they are missing one of their students? It might be a good idea to circulate the image to them too," Burke said. "Now, is there anything more we can do?"

"I could try and follow up on the numbers we found in her pocket. It could be a phone number or something," Moore said.

"Good idea. And when will we have the full forensic report?" Burke said.

"Probably tomorrow now, boss," Moore said.

"OK. Well, let's get to it then. We'll reconvene tomorrow when the pathologist's reports are in. Thanks, everyone."

Chapter Four

Moore went back to her desk and started to work on the numbers that had been found on the victim's body. She started by putting 00 in front of the long number and dialling it on her phone, but it just returned an unobtainable tone. She was wondering what to do next, when her phone sprung to life.

"Moore," she said.

"Hi, Fiona, it's Ruth here from forensics. Have you got a minute?"

"Yes, sure. Hello, Ruth. What have you got?"

"It's about that tyre track you found out near where the dead girl was discovered. You were right, it is from a motorbike, but there's more."

"Go on."

"It turns out it's quite a specific pattern. One of the guys here is a motorbike nut, and he recognised it. Apparently, it almost certainly belongs to a bike ridden by a Garda."

"Cripes. How do you know?"

"It's a bit of a long story. The Garda use Honda Deauville bikes, or at least some of them do. There were complaints that the rear end of those bikes were a bit skittish with the standard tyres, especially in the wet, so our transport division got onto Honda about it a while back, and a special consignment of Bridgestone Battlax tyres were bought to address the issue. It was a special order, as they weren't on sale generally. They were imported from the factory in Japan. And the pattern you found up near the old factory is from one of those."

"I see. So, the bike could actually be a cop bike, or maybe it was an older one that has been sold on," Moore said.

"Yes, but I don't think it has been sold on. All this happened quite recently, and the transport guys say they haven't had a bike sale for over a year."

"Hmm, I see. OK, Ruth, thanks for that, I think! Of course, it doesn't mean that one of our lads was in any way involved, but it's interesting all the same. Look, keep this to yourself for the moment, won't you? We don't want to start a rumour."

"Don't worry, I won't say a word, but I thought you should know."

"Yes, thanks."

Moore didn't like what she had been told. A quick check on the Garda Personnel IT system revealed that there were around sixty motorcycle Gardaí in the Dublin Metropolitan Division, spread across various sub-divisions such as escort duty, road patrols, speed traps and support for the other divisions, such as the Armed Response Unit. She had no clue as to how she would find out which one of these officers had left their mark close to the scene of an ugly murder, or why.

Feeling quite unsettled, she turned her attention back to the mysterious numbers laid out on the desk in front of her. She stared at the sequence of figures for a few minutes not really seeing them, but then something popped into her head from nowhere. There were 14 numbers in all. Moore had a recollection that some banks used 14-digit account numbers, although it was more common these days to have just eight. But if you tacked the bank's sort code on at the front, that made up 14 characters, which is what Moore was staring at. She turned to her PC.

It was by no means as easy as she had first thought. Several countries use 14-digit bank account numbers, including Estonia, several banks in India, though not all, and some others from around the world too. After a frustrating twenty minutes searching Google and various banking websites, she gave up.

She was sitting at her desk, wondering how to proceed, when her phone rang.

"Is that the officer who is investigating the case of the young woman found along the Royal Canal?" a male voice said.

"Yes, this is Detective Sergeant Fiona Moore. Who is calling, please?"

"Hello, Sergeant. This is Garda Michael Kelleher. I'm in the traffic division based in Phoenix Park. I think I may have seen something that could be of help to you."

"Oh, really? Do you think you could pop in to have a chat, Michael? I'd prefer to get whatever you have face to face."

"Yes, sure. I'm on a day off today. I could be there in half an hour. Store Street, is it?"

"Yes, that's right. I'm in the detective unit on the second floor, but if you ask at the desk, I'll come down."

"Right. See you in a while then."

When the call was ended, Moore went in search of Dónal Lawler. She didn't want to speak to Michael Kelleher on her own, in case what he had to say was important, but neither did she want the officer to think he was being formally interviewed.

* * *

"This is Danny at the front desk, Sergeant. I have a Garda Kelleher here to see you."

"Thanks, Danny, I'll be down right away."

Garda Michael Kelleher was a tall, slim man whom Moore judged to be in his late thirties. He was neatly groomed, with well-cut dark hair, a long, tanned face, and he was wearing pale-coloured chinos, a navy polo shirt, with a waist-length black leather jacket. The two of them shook hands, and Moore lead the way upstairs to an office where Dónal Lawler was waiting. Moore introduced the two men and they all sat down around the desk in the centre of the room.

"Thanks for coming in, Michael. Can I get you a coffee or a cup of tea?" Moore asked.

"No thanks, I'm fine."

"OK, well what is it that you think might be of use to us with this case then?" Moore said.

"Well, the night the woman was supposedly killed, I was on duty, patrolling the roads up near Glasnevin and Phibsboro on the bike. It was quiet enough, but at around ten-thirty I spotted an old Toyota Avensis travelling towards the city with no lights on. I pulled the car over and spoke to the driver. He wasn't Irish, but he had an Irish license and there was no smell of drink off him. He said he had just forgotten to turn his lights on, so I asked him to switch them on, and I checked that the lights at the front and the back of the car were working. Everything was in order, so I sent him on his way, telling him to be more vigilant in future."

"OK. But what has this to do with the murder?" Lawler said.

"Well, here's the thing," Kelleher said. "Yer man had a female passenger in the car. I didn't really see too much of her, I was dealing with the driver after all. But she was upset, and appeared quite nervous. I didn't pay it any mind at the time. The last thing you need when you're on patrol is to get involved in some sort of domestic."

"OK, so what makes you think that this has anything to do with our case, Michael?" Moore said, keen to get to the point, if there was one.

"That's it, you see. Later on – it was coming up to midnight – I was going around the back streets just near the canal, when I see the same car parked up at the side of one of the little side streets, but this time there was just the driver in it. When he saw me, he started the engine and drove off in a bit of a hurry. I did a bit of a tour around the area, which took me up along the tow path of the canal at one point, but found nothing. I thought I might come across the woman if she had legged it from the car and needed help. But it was nearing the end of my shift, so when I'd had a good look around, I went back up to The Park and clocked off."

"Did you go into the old factory, Michael?" Moore asked.

"No, I stayed on the bike. It was all quiet in the area, so I had no reason to investigate. Do you think there's a connection?"

"It's hard to tell. I presume you got the registration number of the Avensis?" Moore said.

"I did of course," Kelleher said. He took his pocket book out of his inside jacket pocket and thumbed through it.

"05-D-126420."

"And have you run the number against the database?" Lawler said.

"Eh, no. I didn't think there was anything in it, to be honest, at least not until I heard about the dead woman."

"OK. Well, we can check that here. Was there anything else that you might have noticed about the driver or the car, or even the passenger, that didn't seem relevant at the time, but could be important? Did you see what she was wearing at all?"

"As I said, I didn't really get a good look at her. I was leaning down from a standing position to talk to the driver through his window. But I can say that she had dark hair, a white shirt and blue jeans. That's about it, I'm afraid."

"Did you take a note of the driver's name, Michael?"

"No. We don't usually do that unless there's something suspicious, and there was nothing to indicate that there was anything wrong. You'd be surprised how many cars we have to stop that don't have their lights on."

"Yes, I'm sure," Moore said. She wasn't terribly impressed with the alertness of the young bike cop, but she admitted to herself that hindsight was of little help in these cases.

"Can you hang on here while I go and check the registration number of the Avensis, Michael?" Lawler said.

"Yes, of course. Do you think it was her in the car?"

"Your description fits, all right. It could well have been," Moore said.

"Christ! And yer man might have just killed her, and there I was letting him get away," Kelleher said despondently.

"You weren't to know. Don't beat yourself up. We have more information than we had this morning in any case, thanks to you."

Moore and Kelleher chatted for a few minutes about nothing of importance. Then Lawler came back into the room.

"It's a non-existent number, I'm afraid," he said. He sat down again at the desk. "The 05-D numbers stopped at 109,419, and the ones over a hundred thousand are all UK imports."

"God, I'm sorry, folks. I never thought," Kelleher said.

"It can't be helped. But can you put out a bulletin about the vehicle for us? And put a stop and detain notice on the driver as a person of interest. You never know, we might just get lucky," Moore said.

"Yes, OK, and I'll have a good look around myself up in that area too when I'm back on duty."

Chapter Five

First thing the following morning Moore went to find Burke. He was in his office, looking glum and distracted.

"Hi, boss. Everything OK?" Moore said. She was not used to seeing her boss quite so preoccupied.

"Not really, Fiona, no."

"Do you want to talk about it?"

"Come in. Close the door."

Moore did as she was asked and took a seat opposite Burke.

"Do you remember that business with the woman from European Airways, Andrea, the co-pilot a few months back?" Burke said.

"Yes, of course. Why, what's up?"

"Well, someone has put in a complaint against me over it. Heffernan is going mad. I had a meeting with him yesterday, and he tore the arse out of me."

Jerome Heffernan was their superintendent. He had overall charge of the detectives attached to Store Street, and was generally supportive, but somewhat intolerant if he thought there was anything untoward going on amongst the team. He was originally from Cork in the south of the country, and came to Dublin when the only opening he could get as superintendent was in the capital city. But he hadn't lost any of his Cork ways.

Burke looked at his sergeant directly.

"It wasn't you, was it?" he said.

"Jesus, boss! How could you even think such a thing? For God's sake, you know I'd never do anything like that," Moore said, her face reddening with indignation.

"Yes, sorry. It's just I'm at my wits' end. If I knew who it was that grassed me up, I might be able to deal with it. But the way it is, I could be looking at a serious disciplinary, or worse."

"Can Heffernan not smooth it over for you?"

"He doesn't know. It's gone to GSOC. He has some good contacts in there. Apparently one of the senior men worked with him in Cork when he was a lowly sergeant, and they were quite close. But I don't know how far he is prepared to stick his neck out to save my sorry ass."

"Was she worth it, boss?"

"Feck off, Moore. Christ, sometimes I wonder about you!"

"Ah, I like to keep people guessing, that's all."

"Anyway, what have you got on this woman by the canal, or did you just come in for a chat?"

Moore told Burke about the visit of Michael Kelleher.

"Hmm, not very bright is our Garda Kelleher, is he? Still, I suppose coming up to the end of your shift on a cold night, I might have done the same. What did you think of him?"

"I'm not sure. I'm going to have a little snoop around about his background, his track record, that sort of thing. I'm sure he's OK, but it's a bit odd that he didn't go into the old factory knowing that it is used as a hang-out. And forensics did say that he stopped the motorbike on the tow path. They found the imprint of the side stand in the soft clay as well as the tyre print."

"Hmm... I see what you mean. Christ, I hope he's not involved. That's all I bloody need right now."

"Let's see what I can dig up. Are you OK now, boss?"

"Ah, yes, I'll survive. But I hope the man above can sort this other business out. I don't fancy being busted down to sergeant and being transferred to Cahirciveen!"

Moore laughed.

* * *

When she got back to her desk, there was a message for her to call a Sergeant O'Reilly in Finglas Garda Station.

"Sergeant O'Reilly? This is Detective Sergeant Fiona Moore here from Store Street. You were looking for me."

"Ah, thanks Fiona. Yes, I was. It's about a silver Toyota Avensis you have been looking for. We got a call early this morning from a woman who lives on one of the estates just off the McKee Avenue, facing that waste ground. There was a car on fire, so we got the fire brigade out to it. Unfortunately, it's not that unusual around here. But the woman had made a note of the registration number before the car was burnt out, and it's on the system with your name attached. There's not much of it left, but there may be something useful in the remains."

"Right, well thanks for the call. Could you tape off the wreckage and get someone to keep an eye on it? I'll come out with our forensic team in a little while."

"Yes, sure, no problem. I'll get one of the young lads here to mind it for you. What time will you be up?"

"In about forty minutes. Is that OK?"

"Yes, of course. Thanks."

Moore called forensics and asked them to get out to Finglas to examine the burnt-out car. She then went and found Dónal Lawler.

"C'mon, Dónal, let's go. I have a nice Toyota Avensis for you to look at."

They pulled up alongside the area of open ground that O'Reilly had told them about in Finglas. The burnt-out hulk of the car stood at the edge of a patch of grass that was obviously well used by the children of the neighbourhood. Discarded plastic toys lay around, but the main feature was a blackened and singed area that extended about three metres all around the charred wreck. The forensic team were already on site and were all suited up and had started to examine the remains of the car. Moore asked Lawler to call Sergeant O'Reilly and get the name and address of the woman that had called it in, and instructed him to go and talk to her in case she might have information about how the car had arrived, or who had been driving it.

Moore walked up over the well-worn grass to where the car was sitting looking very sorry for itself. An officer in a white suit came across to her.

"Good morning, Sergeant. I'm Philip Maher. We're just starting to go over this one, but there's not much left, I'm afraid."

"Hi, Philip, it's Fiona, by the way. It looks to be well scorched. No chance of any prints, I guess?"

"Not a hope. I'd say whoever set the fire used about three litres of petrol on the seats and interior. There's a badly burnt red plastic jerrycan on the ground beside it."

"Ah, nice. We might be able to trace where that was filled later. Anything at all inside the vehicle?"

Just then, the other forensic officer came across carrying a clear plastic bag with some charred material inside.

"I found this under the passenger's seat. It's a small handbag. It's leather, so it didn't burn very well, and there's stuff inside," the man said, handing it over to Moore.

"OK, thanks. I don't think I'll open it here in case it falls apart. Is it OK for me to keep it?"

"Yes, that's fine. We have it photographed and recorded in any case," the forensic officer said.

"Thanks, if there's anything else of interest give me a bell later. I want to get back into town as soon as my colleague re-appears."

"No problem," Philip said. He turned his attention back to the burnt-out hulk of the Toyota.

* * *

Mrs Maire Connelly was probably in her late seventies, Lawler guessed. She was a small woman with a determined expression on her face that Lawler surmised had seen some tough times.

"Mrs Connelly, I am Detective Garda Lawler. I wonder if I could have a word with you about the car?" he said. He gestured back over his shoulder in the direction of what was left of the vehicle.

"Come in, Detective. Can I get you a cup of tea or something?"

"No thanks. I'll not delay you. I was just wondering what exactly you saw this morning before you called the station?" he said. They were now entering the small front room of the terraced house that Mrs Connelly kept in pristine condition.

"This place used to be so quiet, you know. We moved here at the end of the eighties when they condemned our flat in Sherriff Street. It was very peaceful then, but these days, anything goes. We get one or two of those burnt-out cars every few months now. It's shocking," the old woman said.

"Yes, I'm sure," Lawler said. He was anxious to find out if the woman had seen anything significant. "What time did you see the car at, Mrs Connelly?"

"I was just getting a cup of tea at around seven when I heard it. A big whooshing sound, and then I went to the window here, and there it was, all ablaze. But the back of the car was facing me, and the number was clearly visible. Thank God, I still have my eyesight. I wrote it down on this old envelope here." Mrs Connelly proffered the piece of paper with the number scrawled in pencil, but it clearly showed 05-D-126420 as the registration she had recorded.

"Did you see who arrived in the car at all?"

"No. Whoever it was had run off by then. There was no sign of anyone around. It's always the same. I suppose it was used in a robbery or something. Probably stolen as well. Dirty rascals!"

"And you're sure there was no one hanging around that looked out of place? These chaps often stay to admire their handiwork," Lawler said.

"Not that I could see anyway, and it's wide open over there on the green. If there was anyone, I would have seen them, but there was no one," Mrs Connelly said quite emphatically.

"Ah, OK, yes, of course. Well, that's all I think I need for now, ma'am. Thanks for your help. Should anything else occur to you, you might give me a call." Lawler handed the woman a small card with his details. He said goodbye to Mrs Connelly, and made his way back to Moore who was just finishing up with the forensic team.

"Well, Dónal, what's the story?"

"The woman confirmed that it is the car we are looking for. She took down the registration number before the fire did its thing. But she didn't see the person that drove it up here, or anyone hanging around while it burnt."

"That's something, at least," Moore said.

"Did you get anything?"

"Yes, I did," Moore said. She held up the plastic bag containing the charred leather handbag. "And there's a partly destroyed petrol can as well. We may be able to get something from that. Let's get back to the station and let the lads finish up here."

Chapter Six

Burke had been summoned for a further meeting with his boss, Superintendent Jerome Heffernan. He was certain he knew what the meeting was about, and he wasn't looking forward to it – not one little bit.

"Damn that bloody woman," he said to himself as he ascended the stairs towards Heffernan's office.

He knocked gingerly on Heffernan's door.

"Come in."

"Good morning, sir, you asked to see me."

"Yes, come in, Inspector. Take a seat."

The fact that Heffernan called him by his rank, and not the usual first name, was not a good sign.

Burke sat as he was instructed and waited for Heffernan to give him his attention. The senior man played with papers on his desk, looking down at them, by way of building some tension between the two officers. Eventually, he looked up.

"I wanted to speak to you about this complaint that has been made against you. I need you to tell me the extent of your involvement with this Swedish woman, and how it came about."

Burke thought quickly for a moment before replying.

"Is it getting serious, sir?" he said.

"Never mind that. Just give me the information that I have asked you for, and do it now please. I'm busy."

Burke outlined his brief affair, if you could call it that, with the Swedish pilot in terms that were as benign as he could manage without actually lying.

"I see. And how exactly did this affect the investigation that was underway at the time?" Heffernan said.

"I'd say it was some help in exposing the whole thing, quite frankly, sir."

"How very convenient," Heffernan said. "Right, I'll level with you Aidan. I've spoken to my contact in GSOC. He's sympathetic, but only because it's me that's asking, 'for old times' sake' as it were. He's trying to prevent the matter getting tangled up in the whole procedure that could lead God knows where. It's not just you that could be in trouble over this, you know. I could come under fire too."

"Yes, sir, I'm sorry. What happens now then?"

"I'll have to leave it with him for another week or so to see what he can manage. But you need to be on your very best behaviour till this is resolved, if, in fact, we can get it dealt with without bringing the ceiling down on both of us. These things are extremely sensitive at the moment what with all the accusations in the force of misogyny and harassment of female officers and suspects. You should by rights be suspended, but that would only give weight to the complaint, and I don't want to do that. Not for now, in any case," Heffernan said.

"May I ask you one thing, sir?"

"What?"

"Who was it that filed the complaint?" Burke said.

"I wouldn't tell you even if I knew myself, Inspector. You'll find out in due course if it comes to an official enquiry."

"Yes, but if it was one of my team, I need to know. After all, we are supposed to have complete trust between us. Our lives sometimes depend on it."

"Well, I can't say, and you should put that out of your mind too. It's not helpful. Now go and do your job, and try and keep your hands off the women!" Heffernan said.

Burke got up, and without saying another word, left the room. He was furious.

* * *

Moore and Lawler arrived back in the station late morning.

"Dónal, will you do a sweep of the garages around Finglas? See if they have CCTV of the forecourt, and if so, see if you can get hold of it. We're looking for some dude filling a jerrycan last night. Let me know if you get a hit, OK?"

"Yes, boss. I'm on it."

Moore then went to her desk and placed the plastic bag containing the singed handbag on it. She called Amy Sutton, the junior detective in the team, across.

"Thanks, Amy. I want you to help me with this. Can you get a large sheet of paper or plastic that we can lay out on my desk here? This thing is fragile, and I don't want to lose any of it."

"Yes, sure, give me a minute," Sutton said.

She was back a moment later with a large lump of brown paper. The two of them cleared the surface of Moore's desk, and spread the paper out, covering the entire surface. Moore donned blue vinyl gloves before gently opening the evidence bag and taking out the remains of the leather handbag.

"OK, let's see what we've got."

The outside of the bag was badly scorched. It was black and sooty, but when Moore opened it up, the inside was in much better condition. She reached in, and withdrew the contents. There was a purse, a set of keys, some basic items of makeup, and a Spanish identity card which was buckled from the heat, but still quite legible.

"Ah, at last. Let's see who you are, my friend," she said taking up the identity card which bore a photograph of a young woman with bright eyes and shoulder-length wavy hair.

"Gabriella Ortez, date of birth 20 March 1999. So, she was twenty-two years old, more or less as we thought," Moore said.

"Is there an address on the ID card?" Sutton said.

"Nope, just the date it was issued and the expiry date and a serial number. It was issued two years ago, and is valid for ten years," Moore said.

"That's something to go on, at least. Perhaps the Spanish Embassy would be able to get us an address for her," Sutton said.

"Yes, well we need to notify them in any case. Can you get onto that for me?"

"Yes, of course."

"And then, Amy, I'd like you to keep calling all the English teaching schools in the city and see if our Ms Ortez was attending any of them. If you strike it lucky, get an address," Moore said.

"Right, boss."

"Here, help me tidy up this lot before you go."

* * *

Burke arrived back down from the superintendent's office looking grim. His face was red, and he was in foul form.

"Jesus, boss, you look like you've swallowed a wasp! Is everything OK?" Moore said. She followed him into his office.

"No, it bloody isn't. Sit down there for a minute. We need to talk. I need to know if it was anyone else on the team that dobbed me in. If someone has it in for me, I have to find out."

"I very much doubt it, boss. Surely you can't think it was one of us? More likely the woman herself, trying to get her sentence reduced if you ask me."

"Maybe. But will you do a little digging for me, quietly, needless to say," Burke said.

"I'm not mad about it, but OK, I'll see what the word around here is for you."

"Thanks, Fiona. You're the only one I can really trust at the moment. I appreciate it. Now, to more immediate matters. What's the story on the murder?"

Moore filled her boss in on what had been discovered from the burnt wreckage of the Toyota, and what she was doing to establish where the victim lived.

"Excellent work. It's amazing how something that goes under the seat in the car escapes discovery. My car probably has loads of stuff under there that I've lost over the years!"

"Let's not go there, boss!"

"Right. Well, let me know if Dónal or Amy come up with anything. I've got some thinking to do."

Chapter Seven

At four-thirty that day, Burke brought everyone together for an update.

"Right. Let's see what we've got. Fiona?" Burke said.

"Well, as you know, we recovered the woman's handbag from the burnt-out car. We have an ID for her now – she's Gabriella Ortez, from Spain. Amy, did you get anything from the Spanish Embassy?"

"No, I'm afraid not. They are trying to get an address for her, but they told me that it's not an unusual name, so it could take a while."

"OK. Do you have anything for us, Amy?"

"I've been on to the English schools in the city. To be honest, they were less than helpful. Most of them have only part-time administrators during term time. But now that I have a name, I might make more progress. I'll try again tomorrow," Sutton said.

"Don't take any shit from them. This is a murder enquiry after all. If anyone is being stand-offish, pay them a visit and put the fear of God into them. We need an address for Gabriella Ortez, and soon. Any sign of her mobile phone?"

"Get this. Forensics found no fewer than four mobile phones in the canal. There were SIM cards in two of them. They've sent them up to The Park to the techies up there to see if they can recover anything from any of them, but it will take a day or two," Moore said.

"What about the car? Have we checked for a list of stolen Toyota Avensis machines?" Burke said.

"Eh, no, boss. Do you think we should?" Lawler said.

"Damn right. And while you're at it, see if forensics can get the VIN number off the car. That's usually stamped into the metal, so it won't have been destroyed. What about CCTV from the petrol stations?"

Sensing that Lawler was becoming overloaded, Moore spoke up. "I'll do those tomorrow, boss."

"And did forensics get anything back from the jewellery the girl was wearing?" Burke said.

"No, boss, nothing. Sorry," Moore said.

"C'mon, folks. For God's sake, let's get on with this. You know the trail goes cold after a few days. This isn't rocket science. By this time tomorrow I want an address for this woman. I want to know why she was here, and preferably who her known associates were. Who were her friends, did she have any work here, where did she party, had she a boyfriend, or maybe a girlfriend? Let's get serious about this!" Burke said.

The team all looked away, avoiding eye contact with the inspector. Before he left to go back to his office, he said to Moore, "Fiona, a word in my office please."

Moore followed her boss into his office.

"What about Michael Kelleher? Have you looked into his background?" Burke said.

"Jesus, boss, give us a chance. We've been up to our eyes with this thing, and we're pretty tightly stretched. He's hardly a priority, now, is he?" Moore said.

"Don't even think of asking for more resources, Fiona. That's not going to happen. You'll just have to work quicker or work smarter. I'll do the Kelleher thing myself if you can't handle it. OK?"

"Can I go now?" Moore replied, biting her tongue.

"Off you go," Burke said.

Moore was miffed at the way Aidan Burke had treated her. She knew he was going through some personal issues, what with the complaint against him and everything, but she still felt he was being very unfair to her and the team. She got her coat and set off for home determined to find a way to deal with him without getting herself kicked off the force.

* * *

Moore pulled her car up in front of the galvanized iron gates that guarded the entrance to her apartment complex on Mayor Street and blipped the fob to open them. She had moved into the city centre the previous year. It was a very handy location. She could walk to the Point Depot to see a concert, stroll to lots of reasonably priced eateries, and it was convenient for meeting friends for a night out on the town when the occasion arose. The flat came with a dedicated underground car parking space too, and her landlord was responsive when anything needed doing. As a Garda Sergeant, Moore was paid just over €60,000 a year when various allowances were taken into account. But as a single person with no dependents, her tax rate was quite high; still she reckoned that the amount consumed by the rent on her dwelling was worth it.

When the gates had opened fully, she drove in and around in front of her building, then down the ramp into the basement. The lights were supposed to come on when a car entered, but they were quite unreliable, and this time she had only the headlights of her own car to illuminate the area. As she swung the car into her spot, she thought she saw someone disappearing behind a pillar, but she couldn't be sure in the half-light. She got out of the car and walked briskly to the lift, looking around her as she did so, but could see no one.

Once inside, in the safety of her own space, she cooked her evening meal, downed a large glass of red wine, and relaxed in front of the telly until it was time for bed. The wine helped her to sleep soundly, and the next thing she knew her phone was jangling on her nightstand. It was seven-thirty in the morning.

Moore showered, dressed and grabbed a quick scrambled egg and a cup of coffee and left the apartment. She went down in the lift, but when she got to her car, she was horrified at what she saw. Both door mirrors had been smashed to the ground, there was heavy keying all along the driver's side of the vehicle. The windscreen had a long crack going diagonally across it from the bottom right-hand corner, and both headlights were smashed.

Moore looked around anxiously to see if the perpetrator was lying in wait for her but could see nothing. She couldn't drive the car in that condition, so she went back upstairs and called Store Street.

"Hi, Danny. It's Sergeant Moore. Look, my car has been vandalized overnight and is undriveable. It's pretty beaten up, to be honest. Any chance you could get someone down to me? There may be some evidence of whoever did this, and anyway I need a lift to the station."

"Sorry to hear that, Fiona. I'll get a car down to you straight away. Just confirm your address for me."

Moore did the necessary and thanked the desk sergeant. She then called the garage that looked after the squad cars when they got into trouble, which was frequently, and asked them to come and collect it in the afternoon. By that time the Gardaí would have finished gathering any evidence that had been left during the attack. While she was waiting for her lift, she called the landlord and explained the situation.

"Sorry to call you so early, Mr Lynch, but I'm afraid my car has suffered damage in the car park here overnight. I was wondering if you could let me have the CCTV recordings from the front and back of the complex for my colleagues to examine?"

"Sorry to hear that, Sergeant. Yes, of course. I'll get my maintenance man to collect them this morning and have them brought into Store Street for your attention. Is there much damage?" Lynch said.

"Well, it's not driveable. It needs a new windscreen, some body work and two new door mirrors. But it could have been worse."

"I see. Were there any other cars damaged?"

"No, I didn't see any. I think it was targeted."

"I'm sorry. That's upsetting for you. Well look, if it comes to more than €500 let me know. Our insurance will cover it once it's over a certain threshold."

"That's handy. Are you sure?" Moore said.

"Yes, of course. That's why we pay the bloody premiums after all. Might as well get something back from the bloodsuckers."

"OK, well I'll get an estimate later and text it to you if it's over €500. Thanks. And we'll get the CCTV stuff later?"

"Yes, I'll make sure of it."

"Great, thanks again. Bye."

* * *

Moore took a lift back to the station in the squad car while two detectives stayed behind with her car examining it and dusting the gates of the property for fingerprints. They all knew it was more or less a hopeless task, but they had to go through the motions all the same. When she got to the open plan, she bumped into Burke who was walking towards his office with a mug of coffee.

"Morning, boss, sorry I'm a bit late. I had a small drama with my car," she said.

"Yes, I heard. Any idea who was behind it?"

"Not a clue. Anyway, there are two of the lads from Pearse Street going over it before it goes off to the menders," Moore said.

"You haven't had any threats or anything recently then?" Burke said.

"No, nothing like that. But there's some CCTV coming in later from the complex, so we may get a look at chummy then."

"Ah, don't hold your breath. But you never know. Anyway, onwards and upwards. Let me know if anything interesting shows up." Burke went off to his office, cup in hand.

Chapter Eight

Dónal Lawler, now armed with the name of the victim, started helping Amy to call the English schools. Teaching English as a Foreign Language, or TEFL as it was known, had become a big business in Dublin in recent years and there were a lot of them to be contacted. The schools were mostly a few rooms at the top of rickety stairs in old buildings where Irish university students attempted to teach English to people from overseas as a part-time job to supplement their existence. But there were one or two more professional outfits with proper premises and a good number of decent, permanent staff. It was at one of these that Lawler finally scored a hit.

"The World of English, Karla speaking, how can I help you?" the girl said without a hint of an accent to give away her Eastern European origins.

"Good morning, Karla. This is Detective Dónal Lawler from Store Street Garda station. I was wondering if you could tell me if you have a Gabriella Ortez enrolled with you there?"

"Just a moment, I'll look up the roll call for you."

Lawler drummed his fingers on his desk hoping that the sixth call of the day would yield something positive. Karla was back a few moments later.

"Officer Lawler, yes, we have a young woman by that name on our books. She is from Spain, but it looks like she hasn't been in for a few days."

"That figures," Lawler said, not too loudly. "I wonder if I could trouble you for her address here in Dublin?"

"Hold on. Do you think it's OK to give out that information? After all, you might not be from the police," Karla said.

"I can assure you that I am legitimate, Karla. If you like you can look the number of Store Street station up in the phonebook and call me right back."

"I suppose it's OK then. Her address is Flat 3, 128 Moyne Road, Ranelagh."

"That's great, Karla. Thanks for your help."

"Is there anything wrong with Gabriella, officer?"

"Nothing for you to worry about for now, Karla. Just one more thing. Do you happen to have a mobile phone number for her?"

"Hmm... yes, here it is. It's 084 8776445."

"Thanks, Karla, that's terrific. Please don't mention to any of the other students that we were asking about Gabriella for now. We don't want to start any rumours, do we?" Lawler said.

"Of course."

"Thanks again. Bye."

When the call had ended, Lawler used the office phone to dial the number Karla had given him. It rang four times, and was then answered by a male voice who simply said, "Hello."

"This is Detective Sergeant Dónal Lawler. To whom am I speaking, please?"

"Ah, hiya, Dónal. It's Keith Malone here in the Technical Bureau up in The Park. God, you gave me a right fright. We've been drying this thing out for a couple of days along with the others that were fished out of the Royal Canal. I thought it was knackered, but it seems not."

"Hi, Keith. Looks like that's the one that belonged to the murdered woman we found up there. Can you do some work on the SIM and the instrument itself and get a list of calls in the last two weeks for me?"

"Sure. I may have to put a new battery into..."

And with that, the call ended. Seemingly, Keith was right. The phone's battery hadn't enjoyed going for a swim in the murky water, but Lawler was content that Keith had got the message all the same. When he had finished with Keith, Lawler went and found Fiona Moore and updated her with developments.

"That's terrific, Dónal, well done. Can you take Amy and go out to her flat and see what's what? Don't muck the place up. We may need to get forensics out to it. But make a start anyway. See if she lived with anyone. Ask anyone else that's there if they knew anything about her. You know the drill."

"Yes, sure. But I'm supposed to be following up on the burnt-out Toyota too. Can someone else do that for me?" Lawler said.

"Yes, I suppose I'll have to add it to my ever-lengthening list! You get off. And call me if there's anything interesting."

"Right. Chat later."

* * *

Moyne Road was a long, straight road of red-bricked houses that dated from the early part of the twentieth century. Some of the houses were in short terraces of four buildings, while most of them were semi-detached. Over the years, due to the highly desirable location just twenty minutes' walk to the business district in Dublin, the properties had gradually been converted into flats and bedsits. The original occupants moved out over the years to the leafier suburbs, and landlords took over to cash in on the generous rents available.

Number 128 was near the end of the cul-de-sac where a sort of turning circle had been provided for cars. As a result, the front gardens of these houses were truncated, and left barely room for the collection of blue, black and green bins that each house kept for their rubbish out front.

Lawler parked his car in the circle and Sutton and himself got out. They went to the front door of number 128 and saw that there was a stack of six doorbells attached to the wooden doorframe. None of the names in the little plastic windows beside each bell was Ortez, but that didn't surprise them at all. The turnover of tenants in these places was high, and not everyone wanted to be identified in any case.

The two of them were standing at the door when it opened, and a young man with a bicycle squeezed past them without saying a word. Lawler held the door open for him to make things a bit easier, and when the cyclist had departed, the two detectives went inside. Sutton was surprised that the owner had managed to fit six individual dwellings into what was quite a small house. There were two that must have been bedsits on the ground floor, another two on the first floor, one at the back on the return landing, and a sixth in the attic space let into the roof. They knocked on the doors on either side of the entrance hall, and then tried the door handles, but each of those units were firmly locked. On the first floor, the room to the left of the miniscule landing, much of which was now consumed with the stairs to the loft area, stood with the door ajar. Splintered wood on the door frame indicated that the door had been forced, but Lawler couldn't tell if it was recent, such was the general poor condition of the place.

Lawler pushed the door open, and waited before entering carefully, making sure there was no one inside. Despite the partly open door, the room was stuffy. It was very cramped too. There was a single bed along one wall, and the rectangular symmetry of the room had been distorted by the installation of a tiny shower room that just about managed to accommodate a toilet and very small wash-hand basin as well. Along the outside of this arrangement, a kitchenette of sorts was arranged, comprising a small stainless-steel sink, a shelf with a microwave oven, beneath which was a small fridge. There was barely room to stand in the room without bumping into something, and there was simply no room for a wardrobe of any kind.

"God, I wonder how much they pay for this lot. Daylight robbery, whatever it is. Anyway, let's have a look around. We might at least be able to find out if this is where Ortez was staying," Lawler said.

It didn't take them long to discover evidence of the young Spanish woman. On the floor beside the bed there were a few letters addressed to Gabriella Ortez, Flat 3, 128 Moyne Road. Under the bed there was a small suitcase, and Lawler pulled it out onto the floor.

"Don't you think we should get forensics out, Dónal? It looks as if it may have been broken into, and after all, the woman was killed," Sutton said.

"Let's have a quick shuftie ourselves first. Have you got gloves on?"

"Yes. Of course. OK."

Lawler opened the suitcase which contained a few clothes and two pairs of shoes together with a small handbag. He opened the bag and withdrew a Spanish passport. Inside, there was a picture of Gabriella Ortez in happier times, looking unusually radiant for a passport photograph.

"This is our client, all right. But have a proper look around, Amy. She must have had a laptop, and I don't see one here."

Sutton started searching the tiny room, looking in all the less obvious locations for the notebook computer.

Having looked through the bedclothes, under the mattress, in the so-called bathroom, and behind the well-worn curtains, she finally opened the fridge. There, in the vegetable drawer at the bottom of the appliance, was a small grey HP laptop computer, nicely chilled.

"Cripes, I hope this thing is still working. I have no idea if putting it in a fridge would damage it, do you?" Sutton said to her colleague.

"Nope, none. But bag it up and we'll get it up to the techies and see if they can breathe life into it. Don't try and turn it on. I'll bring the passport and these letters. Now let's get out of here. This place is doing my head in."

On the way back to Store Street in the car, Amy Sutton called the Technical Bureau and spoke to Keith.

"Hi, Keith. Listen, we've just recovered the Ortez laptop from the bottom drawer of her fridge. It's nice and cold. What should we do with it?"

"Well don't attempt to turn it on. Bring it to a warm place with plenty of air circulating and leave it for twenty-four hours. Then try and start it. The screen might be buggered, but apart from that it should be OK. If the screen isn't working connect it to an external monitor via a USB or VGA port. The disk should be fine. It's probably an SSD job anyway, and they don't suffer from being cooled."

"I hope someone at the station understands all that gobbledygook, Keith. Can we call on you if we get stuck?" Sutton said.

"Yes, of course. And by the way, her phone is coming along nicely. We should have a list of calls and contacts later on today."

"Great. Thanks."

Chapter Nine

Moore was sitting at her desk staring at the long list of tasks that she had before her. She had to start somewhere, so she rang the forensic team and enquired about the VIN number on the burnt-out Toyota.

"Hi, Keith, it's Fiona Moore. I was just wondering if your folks have any news on the VIN number on the old Avensis from Finglas?"

"Hang on. I'll ask someone."

Moore could hear a muffled conversation going on in the background, and a few moments later, Keith was back on the line.

"Here it is. Have you got a pen?"

"Yes, shoot."

"WBAET76010NK72195. Do you want me to repeat it?"

"No, but I'll read it back to you," Moore said, and called out the number.

"By the way, we looked it up. That vehicle was written off about a year ago as beyond repair. But it looks as if some huckster patched it up and put it back on the road. Whoever was driving it probably bought it for €200 from a scrapyard or something."

"Terrific, Keith, you've made my day," Moore said.

"Sorry."

"Don't worry about it. Thanks anyway."

When the call was ended, Moore's phone rang again almost immediately.

"Hi, Sergeant. It's the front desk here. A man has just left a small package for you. He said you were expecting it," the desk sergeant said.

"Did you get a name?"

"Lynch. He said you know him."

"Oh, yes, right, he's from my apartment complex. I'll come down directly and collect it. Thanks."

A few minutes later Moore opened the small, padded envelope that her landlord had delivered to find two little SD memory cards within. She decided to wait until either Dónal Lawler or Amy Sutton was back to review the footage. She needed four eyes on it.

While she was waiting, she turned her attention to any possible CCTV evidence that might be recovered from petrol stations in the vicinity of where the Toyota had been found. She brought up a website called Pumps.ie which showed where the best value fuel was available in Ireland, and zoned in on the area around Finglas. There were six petrol stations in the immediate area of where the car had been found. One of them was operated by Tesco, but the remaining five were run by the big brand names such as Circle K and Topaz. She was certain that they would have CCTV focused on the forecourt to capture the registration numbers of any motorists that left without paying. Not wanting to trust the retrieval of any possible evidence to anyone else, she decided to drive out there herself and go around the outlets and collect their recordings. Reviewing the CCTV footage from outside her apartment could wait.

* * *

Burke had put a phone call into a colleague that he knew from a previous posting in An Garda Síochána. Inspector Pat O'Grady was now a senior officer in the Roads Policing division in The Phoenix Park. The two had worked together when they were both sergeants, and Burke reckoned O'Grady was sound.

"Hello, Pat. Long time no see. How are you keeping?" Burke said having introduced himself to the man.

"Ah, Aidan. How's it going? We're all pretty good up here, thanks. I'm just about to go out and inspect one of our jeeps that got rammed last night when we were chasing a gang of thugs around Neilstown."

"Oh. Anyone hurt?"

"None of ours, thank God, but some of the young scumbags are probably feeling a bit sore this morning. Our lads were very angry about their nice shiny BMW!"

"Good enough for them. Listen, I was wondering if you know one of your motorcycle cops, a Michael Kelleher?" Burke said.

"Not offhand, but I can have a nosey around and see if anything crops up. Why the interest?"

"Ah, probably nothing. We're investigating the murder of a young woman here in the city, and his name just came into it. Nothing suspicious, but you know how I hate loose ends."

"Oh, OK. Well, leave it with me for a while, and I'll call you back. Good to hear from you, Aidan. We must do a proper catch-up sometime soon."

"Yes, we must. Thanks, Pat. Talk to you later."

* * *

Amy Sutton and Dónal Lawler had arrived back with the computer that they had recovered from the young woman's bedsit. Lawler put it on his desk with the lid open and a 'Do not touch' message written in thick black marker on a yellow Post-it stuck to the front of the keyboard.

Lawler went off to find Burke to bring him up to date with their visit to the woman's accommodation in Ranelagh.

"Well, at least we have a proper ID for her now, and we know why she was here. Was there anything else of interest at her bedsit?" Burke said.

"No, nothing. To be honest, the place was a bit of a tip. And God knows how much she was paying for that dump. It's scandalous the rents these people get away with," Lawler said.

"Do we know who the landlord is?"

"No, but I can look it up on the PRTB website, that's if he's registered at all."

"Do that. Maybe he fancied a bit of a fling with a pretty foreign student, and it all got a bit out of hand. Who knows?" Burke said.

"Anything else, boss?"

"No, not at present. Fiona has gone off chasing CCTV from the petrol stations to see if we can get a clip of our lad filling his jerrycan. I'm waiting for information to come through on our friendly motorcycle cop. How long do you think you'll have to leave the frozen laptop for before we can power it up? That could hold some really valuable clues as to what happened to the poor lass."

"It should be OK by tomorrow."

"OK. Let me know when you get it going."

"Right, will do."

* * *

Moore was very successful in her harvesting of CCTV footage from the petrol stations that she had targeted. They all had a system for retaining DVDs of the recordings for a month at least, and most of them had some sort of rudimentary filing system in place too. As she was able to give an accurate date for the ones she was interested in, it didn't take her long to round up five DVDs and get back into town.

"OK, folks," she said when she had fetched a coffee for herself and was seated in the open plan, "we've got some serious viewing coming up. Dónal, can you take the DVDs from the petrol stations and see if you can spot our man buying the fuel to set his car on fire? Amy, I'd like you to come with me and watch the CCTV from outside my apartment. Are we all OK to stay on it till we've seen it all?" she said.

"Yes, boss," they all replied in unison.

"Right. Let's get to it then."

Amy Sutton got herself a coffee too, and herself and Moore sat down at Moore's PC where an adapter had been fitted to accommodate SD cards. Moore used the VLC program to access the contents of the little storage devices. The first one was a street view, largely focused on the main entrance to the complex. The camera must have had a motion sensor on it, as it only recorded when there was movement in its field of vision. They watched as several cars arrived back at the gates between six-thirty and eight o'clock, including Moore herself.

"There. That's you going in, Fiona. Another late shift by the looks of it."

"Naturally," Moore said smiling.

They continued to watch, but the comings and goings became fewer as the time wore on, so it wasn't as arduous as it might have been. As the time stamp went past 1:00 a.m., Amy let out an expletive.

"Shit! Stop it there. Go back a few seconds. Do you see what I see?"

Moore wound the video back a few frames. Just at the edge of the screen, almost out of range, they both saw what was clearly a motorcycle passing the gate at a very slow pace. The video was in black and white, so it wasn't possible to determine the colour of the bike. The driver appeared to be scanning the entrance as he drove past. The camera hadn't captured the registration number of the bike either, and of course it didn't have a front number plate at all.

"Interesting!" Moore said.

"It could be innocent enough. They probably patrol that area quite a bit at night in any case," Sutton said.

A few minutes later, a person dressed all in black appeared on the film. He, if it was a man, climbed easily over the pedestrian entrance to the apartments, and skulked away on the far side of the gate towards Fiona Moore's block. The time stamp showed that the intruder was only inside for six minutes, and he then exited through the pedestrian gate again, this time being able to release it from inside using the button provided.

"Wow! Do you reckon that's our man?" Sutton said.

"Looks like it."

"Do you reckon it was a cop on the bike?"

"Impossible to say. It looks like the right kind of machine. He would have had to ditch his high-vis gear somewhere while he did the deed, but it could have been him. Tell you what, why don't you contact the Roads Policing folks, and see if our friend Kelleher was working last night, and if so, what time he clocked off?"

"Right. Cripes, I hope it's not him."

Chapter Ten

Dónal Lawler was wading through the CCTV that Moore had retrieved from the petrol stations. Unlike the clips Moore and Sutton were watching, the ones Lawler was viewing were continuous, so it took a lot more time. He had selected the DVD from the Circle K station on The North Road in Finglas, as he thought that being close to the M50, it was the most likely place the arsonist would have chosen to buy the accelerant. He wasn't wrong.

The film that Lawler was viewing was split vertically in two. The left pane showed the forecourt, while the right-hand one was from inside, facing into the shop from behind and above the cashiers. There, as clear as day on the footage he was watching, a silver Toyota Avensis pulled up to the pumps. A young man wearing a sweatshirt and jeans with a baseball cap pulled well down over his face got out, went to the boot of the car, and took out a red plastic container which he proceeded to fill with unleaded petrol. Having dispensed the fuel, he put the container back in the boot and went inside to pay. Unfortunately, due to the baseball cap, and the angle of the camera, there was no view of the man's face at all. But this could easily be the person they were looking for. Lawler made a note of the time and resolved to interview the cashier at the location as soon as possible, in case he remembered the customer for any reason.

Lawler found Moore at her desk in the open plan and passed on the information that he had gleaned from the CCTV.

"Do you think we should go out and talk to the cashier?" he said.

"Yes, I do. He's probably on duty now too. It won't take us long to get out there at this time. C'mon, let's go," she said. She grabbed her jacket from the back of her chair, picked up her phone and handbag, and headed for the car park.

* * *

Twenty minutes later Moore pulled her car onto the forecourt of the filing station and parked in the bay that was normally used for people checking their car's tyre pressure. The station was busy, with all of the pumps occupied, and a few more customers in the expansive shop that sold everything from sandwiches to wine and all sorts of other stuff. The two detectives waited in line for the customers ahead of them to complete their transactions. When they got to the head of the queue, Moore showed the cashier her warrant card and asked if he had been on duty the night before last.

"Yes, I came on at six and was here till we closed up at four in the morning," the man replied.

"Is there somewhere we could have a chat? Maybe your colleague here could take over for a few minutes, we won't keep you long," she said.

"Yes, OK," the young man said, a little cautiously.

"Asif, can you take over for a few minutes?" he said to the other cashier.

Asif wasn't best pleased, but agreed all the same.

Outside, Moore asked the man his name.

"I am Kabir. Am I in trouble, officer?"

"No, not at all. We just wanted to ask you about a customer that filled a petrol can here quite late the other night. I was wondering if you remember anything about the man?" Moore said. She produced a still photograph that Dónal Lawler had copied down from the CCTV footage and showed it to Kabir.

"It's not a very good picture. But yes, I remember him, all right. We don't like people filling up cans like that. Of course, we can't stop them. That would require me to leave the shop, and I'm not allowed to do that. But when he came in to pay, I asked him what it was for."

"And?" Lawler said.

"He said it was for his lawnmower. I thought it was odd, because you don't use a lawnmower in the middle of the night," Kabir said.

"Can you remember if he paid in cash or with a card, Kabir?" Moore said.

"That's another thing. He paid in cash. A nice new €50 note. I thought that was a bit unusual too. You don't see many of those in this place, and the fuel was only €4 and a few pence. It was the minimum that those pumps will dispense. Just three litres."

"That's very helpful, Kabir. Tell me, have you ever seen this guy in the shop before?" Lawler said.

"I don't think so. Of course, he may have been here, we don't pay too much attention unless there's something unusual. Are you sure I'm not in trouble?"

"No, don't worry, Kabir. You have been very helpful. Thank you. We'll let you get back, but can I ask if you see this person in the shop again, please call me at once on this number," Moore said, handing Kabir a business card. "It's very important that we know immediately."

Back in the car, Moore let out an expletive. "Shit! We missed that, didn't we?"

"What's that, Sarge?"

"A nice crisp €50 note – that's what. We never found Gabriella's bank card, did we? And tenner bets that's where yer man got the cash. When we get back to the station get onto the banks and see if you can find out about her cash card, when and where it was last used and so on. Damn! Burke will be livid!"

"Ah, don't worry. I think he has more to worry about, don't you?" Lawler said.

"How do you mean?"

"Well, isn't there a complaint in about him and that tasty little Swedish girl?" Lawler said, smirking.

"Oh. How did you find out about that, Dónal?"

"It's all around the station. Worst-kept secret of the week."

"And who exactly told you about it?" Moore said.

"I couldn't possibly say, even if I could remember."

"Shit, Dónal. That's dynamite. If I were you, I'd forget all about anything you may have heard. It's probably not true anyway. And if there is something in it, we need to support the boss, not add fuel to the fire. OK?"

"Yes, Sarge, I hear you."

Moore went quiet. I wonder, she thought to herself as they made their way back to Store Street.

* * *

Lawler went off to chase up the banks to see if he could get any information on Gabriella Ortez's cash card, though he wasn't hopeful, given that it was now well past closing time. But he thought he might make some headway with the twenty-four-hour emergency helpline, and anyway, he needed to earn some brownie points with Moore.

Moore had just settled down at her desk when Aidan Burke came out of his office. He was quite agitated.

"Where the hell have you been?"

Moore explained where they had gone and what they had discovered, which seemed to placate the senior officer somewhat.

"Well, you'd better come into my office. There have been developments."

Burke turned and stomped off towards his office without waiting for Moore to respond. She wasn't looking forward to the next few minutes. When they were both seated at opposite sides of Burke's desk, Moore waited patiently for her boss to speak, but he didn't seem inclined to. Eventually, she broke the tense silence.

"So, what are these new developments then?"

Burke looked up and stared at Moore for what seemed like an age. Then he said, "We may have another one."

"Sorry, boss, another what?"

"Another missing young woman. I had a call about half an hour ago from a man who said his girlfriend hadn't turned up to school today, and he was concerned. He can't reach her on her phone either."

"OK. What has he done so far? Called all her friends? Been around to her place?" Moore said.

"Yes, all of the above. But there's more. The girl is Spanish, and the 'school' in question is The World of English. The same place that Gabriella was attending."

"Did you ask this caller to come in for a chat?"

"Yes, of course. He's a teacher at the school, and he has classes. But he'll be in soon after eight when he's finished."

"OK. What's his name?"

"Hang on," Burke said. He consulted a jotter on his desk. "Peter Ledwidge. He's a modern languages graduate at Trinity, doing his masters."

"Hmm, that's a bit off, isn't it? I mean a teacher going out with a student. It wouldn't have happened in my day," Moore said.

"I think it's a bit different when the student is a grown-up, Fiona. And anyway, I doubt if any of your teachers would have been bothered with you!" he said, smiling.

"Thank you very much, Inspector. I'd forgotten your love life is such a howling success."

"Touché! OK, let's see what he has to say when he gets here. Can you hang around?"

"Eh, let me see. Brad Pitt wanted me to go to dinner with him tonight, but I guess he'll just have to wait. Fancy a coffee?"

"Oh, yes please, and is there anything to eat? I'm starving."

"I'll pop across the road and see what I can find. Back in a few minutes."

"Thanks. Do you need some money?"

"No, you're OK. My treat."

Chapter Eleven

Moore and Burke had finished their coffee and sandwiches when the desk sergeant called up to say that Peter Ledwidge was in reception to see Inspector Burke.

"I'll nip down and get him. Where do you want him?" Moore said.

"Let's keep it informal for now. Show him up here and we'll have a chat."

Moore went off to collect Ledwidge and was back a few minutes later.

Peter Ledwidge was a tall, slim man with a baby face and a mop of curly blonde hair. He was dressed casually in an open-necked shirt and beige chinos with a wine-coloured jacket that Moore felt clashed with the rest of his outfit. She introduced him to Burke and they all sat down.

"Now, Mr Ledwidge, tell us about your concerns for your girlfriend then," Burke said.

"Well, we're not really that much of an item, but we have been out a few times. She's really nice."

"What's the woman's name, Peter?" Moore said.

"Oh, sorry, yes, of course. Alicia. Her full name is Martina Alicia Navarro, but she goes by Alicia. She's from Alicante. She's only been here a few weeks, but we kind of hit it off at once. I don't usually go out with the women from the English school, but we just clicked, so I made an exception."

"Can you give us Alicia's address and mobile number, Peter?" Moore said.

"She has a bedsit on Capel Street over the Polish supermarket. It's a bit of a dump, to be honest, but it's cheap, and it's a handy location." As he was speaking, he wrote down the young woman's mobile number and the address on Moore's notebook.

"Have you been down to Capel Street to see if she's at home?" Burke said.

"Yes, I popped down at lunch time, but there was no response to the bell, and I couldn't get into the building."

"Have you spoken to her friends?" Moore said.

"Yes, I have. The Spanish are a gregarious lot. They all gang around together. But none of them have seen her or heard from her since yesterday when classes finished."

"What time was that?" Burke said.

"Let's see, probably around six o'clock."

"I presume you have heard about the other young woman from The World of English, Peter," Moore said.

"Yes. Gabriella. That's why I contacted you. I'm quite worried about Alicia."

"Can you tell us who she was particularly close to at the school?" Burke said.

"Let me see. Oh, yes, herself and two other Spanish girls gang around together. That's Maria Gomez and Isabella Hernandez, or Izzy, as most people call her."

"Do you happen to have contact details for those students, Peter?" Moore said.

"No, I'm sorry. But you can get the information from the school in the morning."

"And where were you last night, Mr Ledwidge?" Burke said.

"I was teaching at the English school till seven o'clock. Then I went to Grafton Street and got something to eat.

After that I was in the Trinity Library studying till just after eleven when the library closed. I have rooms in College, so I went there and went to bed."

"Do you share your rooms in College, Peter?" Moore asked.

"No. I'm a scholar, so I get a room to myself."

"So, is there anyone that can corroborate your version of last night's events?" Burke said. It was clear he hadn't warmed to the man.

"Now, wait just a minute. You can't think I had anything to do with this. That's preposterous! I'm trying to help you here, for God's sake."

"I take it that's a 'no' then?"

Ledwidge calmed down a bit.

"There were some people I recognised in the library. You could ask them, I suppose. But after eleven, there's no one."

Burke looked at Fiona Moore and motioned towards the door.

"Right, Mr Ledwidge. Thanks for coming in," she said. "We'll take it from here. I'll show you out."

"Is that it?" Peter Ledwidge said. He got up slowly, looking a bit mystified, and inched towards the door.

"We'll be in touch if we need anything more, Peter. If you hear from Alicia, please let us know at once, won't you?"

"Yes, of course. Good evening, Sergeant."

Moore saw the man off the premises, and then returned to Burke's office.

"What now?" she said.

"Get your coat. We have a house call to make!"

* * *

Capel Street was busy at that hour of the evening. The restaurants all along the street were filling up, and there was a buzz in the air. Burke pulled the car up outside the Polish supermarket, managing to find just a single space in an adjacent loading bay. Beside the brightly lit shop, a rather battered solid wooden door with peeling black paint had a small stack of illuminated doorbells. Burke pressed them all in turn, and after a few minutes they could hear footsteps coming quickly down the stairs, before the door was opened by a young man looking somewhat startled by the visitors.

"We're looking for a Spanish woman, Alicia Navarro. Which unit is she in?" Burke said.

The young man just shrugged, turned around and went back upstairs, leaving the door open for them. The two detectives climbed the stair to the first landing which had three doors. One of the doors which was unlocked gave into a small kitchen that was in a very poor state. The other two doors on the landing were firmly closed and protected by Yale locks. Burke knocked firmly on the door to the left of the stairs and waited.

After a few moments it was answered by a young woman with dark blonde hair, dressed in blue jeans and a white top, but nothing on her feet. As she pulled the door open, the smell of fried food wafted out onto the landing.

"We're looking for Alicia Navarro. Do you know her?"

"No," the woman said.

"Do you live alone here?" Moore asked.

"Yes, who wants to know?"

"We're police," Moore said, holding up her warrant card.

"Yes, I live alone. The room is barely big enough for one. Want to look?" she said, standing back and gesturing with her free arm into the room.

"The woman we are looking for is Spanish. Dark, shoulder-length hair, brown eyes, around 170 centimetres tall."

"Oh, yes, well maybe the girl who lives across the hall. That's what she looks like anyway, and I think the rooms further up are occupied by men."

"Ah, right. Have you seen her recently?" Moore said.

"No, but that's not unusual. We don't know each other, so I rarely see anyone else from the house, except if we bump into each other on the stairs."

"May I ask your name?" Burke said.

"Krystyna, Krystyna Wojcik."

"And what do you work at, Krystyna?"

"I work in a nightclub, why?"

"Thanks, Krystyna. Look, if you see the girl from the other room, please ask her to call us. Here's my card," Moore said.

Krystyna closed the door, and they turned their attention to the other room. Burke knocked hard on the door and stood back. After a few moments, he looked at Moore and said, "Probable cause?"

Moore just nodded.

Burke took a piece of flexible plastic that had been cut from an empty salt tub, and slipped it into the door jamb just at the lock. He jiggled it a bit, and the door opened. Before entering, they both donned vinyl gloves.

The room was cramped, but orderly and neat. There was nowhere to prepare food, but it did have a bed with a clean duvet and pillow, an easy chair, a flat screen TV, and a small wardrobe with a drawer in its base. A little white bedside locker had a lamp on it, and when Moore opened the drawer, she found a couple of letters in air mail envelopes with Spanish stamps addressed to Alicia Navarro.

"Sir," Moore said, holding up the envelopes, "looks like this is our woman."

"Right. Well, let's have a quick look around. See if you can spot a phone or a PC or anything useful like that."

Burke and Moore were well practiced in searching a premises. It only took them a few minutes to give the place a good going-over. Before they finished, Burke said, "Open one of those letters and take a photograph of the address on your phone. See who it's from too."

"OK, boss." Moore took out her phone, opened up the topmost letter on the nightstand, snapping it with her mobile phone. Then she folded the letter and replaced it carefully in the envelope, and put it back in the drawer.

On the way back to the station, Moore asked Burke what they should do next.

"We launch a full-blown missing persons case first thing tomorrow. Get back onto The World of English and see if you can get a photo of her. They must have student cards or something with pictures, or maybe Ledwidge has something on his phone. We should have asked him that earlier," Burke said.

"Yes, I never thought of it. Do you think he's involved?" Moore said.

"I doubt it. After all, he came to us, remember?"

"That doesn't mean anything. I get the feeling he's OK. But no harm to do a background check on him all the same, just in case."

Burke dropped Moore off at Store Street and continued on home by himself. Moore decided to go in to see if there had been any developments whilst they had been chasing up the second Spanish woman. When she got inside, she spotted a message for Burke to call Pat O'Grady about Garda Kelleher, but realised that the man would have gone off duty by now, so that was best left till the morning. She also saw that Ortez's laptop PC was sitting on Dónal Lawler's desk, with its power pack plugged in, but she dared not go near it in case it was still thawing out. Left with nothing else to do, she went home herself, walking down through the IFSC to her apartment.

Chapter Twelve

As soon as Aidan Burke arrived at Store Street the next morning, he was contacted by the superintendent's PA. Heffernan was in, and wanted to see him. Burke climbed the stairs in some trepidation. He had no idea what was coming, but he felt that being summoned at this early hour was not a good omen. He knocked a little gingerly on his boss's door.

"Come in," came the more robust response from within.

"Ah, Aidan, come in, take a seat," Heffernan said.

"Good morning, sir. How are things?" Burke said a little tentatively.

"Ah, you know, so-so. Look, I've had a call from my friend in GSOC about this complaint of yours."

"Oh, what's the story?"

"He's managing to keep the lid on things for now, but he said it would be very helpful if you were transferred to another region in the force for a while. That way they could say that positive action had been taken if anything blew up."

Burke couldn't believe what he was hearing. He was a Dublin man, and always had been. He grew up in the city, was educated by the Christian Brothers in the capital, joined the Gardaí and was posted to a station in Irishtown, just two and a half miles to the south of Nelson's Pillar. That was as far away from Dublin as Burke ever wanted to be.

"I see. Where have you got in mind?"

"I still have a few contacts in Cork. I could probably find a spot for you in the city, or maybe Youghal or Kinsale or somewhere nice by the seaside. I'll do whatever I can to keep your present rank of course, but that will depend on manning levels wherever you end up."

"Is this a done deal, sir?"

"No, it's not. Obviously, we would need your consent and you'd have to travel down and meet the superintendent in wherever to see how you got along, but I'd urge you to give it some serious thought, Inspector. If this business with the Swedish woman blows up in our faces, we'll all be looking for a transfer, or worse!"

"How long would I be in exile for?" Burke said.

"Don't be so melodramatic, Aidan. There's nothing at all wrong with Cork, but to answer your question, maybe a year or two. Then we'd get you back here, but it might have to be in another station. Maybe Pearse Street or Fitzgibbon Street."

"I see. When do I have to decide?"

"I can give you a few days. We have to act quickly to be sure we are seen to have been decisive if it all comes out in the wash. Let me know after the weekend," Heffernan said. He then looked down at his desk and started pouring over some papers, which was an indication that the meeting was over.

Burke got up and left, feeling quite shell-shocked.

If the pubs had been open that early in the morning, Burke would have gone straight there and downed a couple of pints and a whiskey or two to steady himself. The information imparted by Heffernan had spooked him badly. He had of course been to Cork a few times. He and his wife Deirdre had gone on holiday to Kinsale once when they were first married, and they had driven into Cork city and visited Fota Island Wildlife Park and walked around through the narrow streets browsing the shops. His memory of the place was somewhat tainted by the fact that he was now separated from his wife, but he could recall the strong accents of the natives, which sometimes made them difficult to understand for someone not from the area.

"Christ on a bike, I'd not last six months down there," he said to himself as he retreated back down to the sanctuary of his own office.

* * *

Burke was settled at his desk pondering the meeting that had just taken place when his phone rang.

"Burke," he said.

"Hello, Aidan. It's Pat O'Grady here. I'm just getting back to you about Garda Michael Kelleher."

"Good morning, Pat, yes thanks. Anything to report?"

"Well, something I suppose. Kelleher hasn't always been a motorcycle cop. He was working in Donnybrook as a uniformed officer, and apparently there was some bit of a story about him making unwelcome advances towards a female Garda when they were out in the patrol car. Nothing much came of it, but soon after, he transferred to the motorbike squad where he would be operating on his own much of the time."

"I see. Was there a formal complaint?"

"No, nothing like that. But you know the way things are these days. Once those sorts of rumours start, they're very hard to shake off."

"Yes, I know exactly what you mean," Burke said, thinking of his earlier meeting. "And has there been anything else since, as far as you know?"

"No, that's it. And there's nothing on his record or anything, but the Super in Donnybrook thought it best to nip things in the bud, so to speak. So, keep what I've told you to yourself, won't you?" O'Grady said.

"Yes, of course. Thanks very much, Pat, that's very helpful. I owe you one."

"No trouble, Aidan. Talk soon."

When the call was over, Burke went out into the open plan to find his sergeant.

"Hi, Fiona. Can you come in for a minute? We need to talk."

"Yes, sure, boss."

When they were seated in his office, Burke relayed the information that Pat O'Grady had given him about Kelleher.

"Hmm... interesting, boss," she said.

"Have you been able to get anything more off the CCTV outside your place?"

"No. It's just not clear enough. But I'm still checking a few things," Moore said.

"Right. Well, what's the story on the missing Spanish woman?"

"We're just getting started on it. I mean, officially, she's not actually a misper yet, but it's a fierce coincidence, isn't it?"

"Coincidence my backside. We'd better step this up a gear, or we'll be looking at another dead body, mark my words. What else is happening?"

"Dónal should be able to start up the laptop we found in the dead Spanish woman's fridge this morning. That may give us something. And we might get her phone records back from forensics today too. They managed to dry out the phone and Keith says he should be able to access it."

"OK, we'll get a photograph of the second woman and circulate it to all the stations in the area. We might get a slot on the one o'clock news as well. You know the drill, 'Gardaí are concerned about what's-her-name. If anyone knows anything about her or where she may be staying, could they please contact us blah blah'. You'd better get around to that English school as well and talk to her friends."

"Right, boss. What are you going to do?" Moore said.

"I have some thinking to do, Fiona, some serious thinking."

Moore sensed that there was definitely something major going on in her boss's world, but she had the good sense not to enquire further. He would tell her in his own good time, or maybe not.

She went back outside and spoke to Dónal Lawler.

"Hi, Dónal. Do you think you could see if that laptop will boot up this morning? If you can get it going, have a look at the emails and the browser history, her bookmarks, that kind of thing. If you find anything significant, call me."

"Right. Are you going out?"

"Yes. I'm going to take Amy and go calling on The World of English. I need to brush up on my past participles," she said, smiling.

"Grand. Catch you later then."

Chapter Thirteen

The World of English occupied an entire three-storey building on Nottingham Street. It had been built in the 1990s when a series of old garages and sheds had been acquired by a developer and bulldozed. A functional modern concrete and glass edifice had been erected in their place. There were four concrete steps up to the entrance, and all around the outside of the premises on the narrow footpath, students milled around smoking and chattering in a variety of foreign tongues.

There was no available parking anywhere on the narrow street, so Sutton had to pull into a laneway between two terraces of red-brick houses, lined on both sides with double yellow lines. She placed her laminated 'Garda on Duty' sign in the windscreen to deter eager parking wardens, if any were skulking about, and Moore and herself walked back to the building.

The reception area was small but functional, festooned with posters advertising local events, and there was a brochure rack mounted on the only solid wall carrying pamphlets of the various courses the place had to offer. Seated at the rather stylish reception desk there was a pretty young woman with long blonde hair tied back in a ponytail. A badge pinned to her expensive-looking white blouse announced her as 'Karla'.

Moore approached, holding up her warrant card for Karla to inspect.

"Good morning, Karla. My name is Detective Sergeant Fiona Moore, and this is my colleague, Detective Garda Amy Sutton. We'd like to speak with whoever is in charge here, please."

"May I ask in what connection please, Sergeant?"

"Could you just get the manager for us? It's quite urgent."

Karla pouted a little, but lifted the phone on her desk and dialled a number.

"Sorry to disturb you, Mrs Walker, but there are two police officers here asking for you."

The detectives couldn't hear Mrs Walker's response, but a moment later, Karla hung up the phone and said, "Mrs Walker will be with you in a few minutes if you'd like to take a seat." Karla gestured to a row of six moulded plastic chairs that were fixed to an aluminium frame and bolted to the floor with their backs to one of the large plate-glass windows that overlooked the street.

As Moore and Sutton sat waiting for the principal to make herself available, the hubbub of the students continued all around. The place seemed to be dominated by Spanish, though there was a good sprinkling of Italians and Koreans as well. The school also seemed to be quite unbalanced from a gender perspective. There were many more females than males attending, or so it appeared from the throngs passing through the reception area all gabbling in their native tongues.

"Sergeant Moore?" said a very tall, painfully thin woman with short, dark curly hair and a mean-looking face.

"Yes. Mrs Walker, I presume."

"Yes, of course. Come along with me, please," the woman said. She turned away and set off walking briskly down one of the long, narrow corridors. Moore looked at Sutton and rolled her eyes to heaven. After a few sharp turns to the left and right, the three of them arrived at an office with a label on its exterior declaring 'Mrs E Walker, Principal'.

Mrs Walker unlocked the door with a key, and proceeded into the room. It was quite spacious, with a window that looked out onto a lane running along behind the building. The window was furnished with vertical blinds, a few of which had abandoned their moorings, and lay awkwardly on the low windowsill. Walker took her natural place behind her desk, and issued the single instruction 'sit' to her guests. The two detectives obeyed.

"Mrs Walker, you will be aware that one of your students was found dead in a derelict building up along the canal recently," Moore said. "We are investigating her death."

"Yes, I heard. But what do you think that has to do with me, or the school for that matter? Obviously, it's terrible for the poor girl and her family, but it has nothing to do with us."

"How do you know, Mrs Walker?" Sutton asked.

"Of course it hasn't. We just do our best to teach them English. We make it perfectly clear in our prospectus that tuition is the only service we provide. God knows, we have enough trouble with regulations, health and safety, Revenue and everything else to keep me fully occupied. My only concern is what goes on in this building. After that, they have to look after themselves. As I am sure you are aware, officer, when young Spanish women get away from their families and come to Dublin, it's probably the first time they have been away from home, and they get up to all sorts, believe me."

Moore decided to try another tack.

"What did you know of the murdered girl, Mrs Walker?"

"Very little, Sergeant. Ortez, wasn't she? She's been here about two months and had moved onto the Intermediate level classes. Her fees were up to date. That's about it, I'm afraid."

"You didn't know her personally then?" Moore said.

"No, of course not. Look, Sergeant, we have something like 300 students attending here what between full-time and part-time. I can hardly be expected to be on one-to-one terms with them all, now, can I?"

"So, Gabriella didn't come to your attention for any reason?"

"No, not at all. I have her file here. It's all perfectly in order, if you'd like to see?" Mrs Walker said. She indicated a brown manila folder on her desk with the number 16401 written in heavy black marker on its face.

"Who would have been Gabriella's tutor, Mrs Walker?" Sutton asked when her colleague expressed no interest in the file being offered.

"There would be more than one. At Intermediate level we start to introduce the students to some of the delights of English literature. You know, Shakespeare, Swift, Yeats and so on. There are separate tutors for the basics and the literature."

"I'd like a list of all the tutors who taught Miss Ortez in the recent past please, Mrs Walker, together with their contact details. And while we're about it, are you aware that a second Spanish student attending here seems to have gone walkabout too?" Moore said.

"No, no I hadn't heard that. What's her name?" Walker said.

"We didn't say if it was a woman, Mrs Walker."

"Eh, no, well, I just assumed," the woman said. She flushed a little, but Moore wasn't sure if that was because she had made an uncharacteristic error, or if there was perhaps more to it.

"Martina Alicia Navarro is her name. Could you pull up her file too, please?" Moore said.

"I'll have to go next door. Excuse me for a minute."

Walker got up and left the room, closing the door behind her.

"What do you make of our headmistress then, Amy?" Moore said.

"Christ! I'm glad she wasn't around when I was at school, that's for sure. She's a tough cookie."

"Yes, but do you think she knows anything about the girls?" Moore said.

"Probably a bit more than she's letting on. Let's wait to talk to the teachers before we jump to any conclusions."

Before they could say any more, Mrs Walker returned clutching another manila folder.

"Here you go," she said, thrusting the file at Moore.

"Is Navarro in the Intermediate group as well?" Sutton asked.

"Here, let me see," Walker said. She reached out and took the file back and opened it.

"Yes, she is in Intermediate too. Why is that important?"

"It could be. Would she have had the same teachers as Ortez?"

"Yes, I imagine so."

"Right. Can we have copies of those two files, please? And we need to speak to two other students – Maria Gomez and Isabella Hernandez."

"If you'd just like to wait outside, I'll get the secretary to make the arrangements," Walker said.

The two detectives got the feeling that they were being dismissed for being naughty.

* * *

When Moore and Sutton were once again seated on the plastic chairs along by the window, Moore said to her colleague, "Look, can you contact the station. Talk to Dónal. See if the other young woman has turned up. If not, we need to escalate things. Do it outside. I don't want us to be overheard. I'm going to get the details of the teachers of the classes these two were attending. We may need to interview them as well."

"Right, boss."

"And if there's anyone with some spare time back at the nick, get them to do a deep dive on this place and her ladyship. There must be some kind of connection."

"OK. I'll come and find you when I'm done."

Amy Sutton went out to make the call while Moore waited for the secretary to arrive with the files. After a few minutes that seemed longer, a woman in her early forties with short blonde hair dressed in a smart, dark-coloured business suit came marching along the corridor, her sensible shoes making a clip-clop sound on the tiled floor.

"Sergeant Moore, I presume," the woman said.

"Yes, and may I know your name, please?"

"Janet, Janet O'Sullivan. I'm the school's secretary. Mrs Walker said you needed these files."

"Yes, thanks, Janet. Oh, and I need to know the names of the teachers that Gabriella Ortez and Martina Navarro were attending."

"Oh, right. By the way, the Navarro girl is known as Alicia, not Martina. The Spanish often do that. She is quite proficient in English. We put her into the Intermediate group more or less straight away when she arrived. To be honest, I'd say she is here to get away from home for a few weeks," O'Sullivan said as they walked back along the seemingly endless corridor to the administrative office beside Mrs Walker's study.

"Did you know either of them at all?" Moore said.

"Yes, a little."

Janet O'Sullivan stopped walking and looked up and down to make sure that there was no one within earshot.

"Look, Sergeant. I know Mrs Walker presents as a rather cool character when you meet her first, but believe me she is a very caring woman. Although she has no obligation, she tries to look after the welfare of everyone here as best she can. It's not easy. Some of these students, especially the young women, get themselves into all sorts of pickles. You see, most of them are not used to being away from home, so Mrs Walker is a kind of surrogate mother to some of them, especially the more naïve ones." She turned back and started walking again.

"And were these two in particular in need of some maternal guidance, do you think?"

"Well, I don't like to speak out of turn, but in the circumstances, I suppose it's OK. Yes, they were. Gabriella was very good-looking. Classic Spanish beauty. Long, dark hair, big brown eyes that always sparked and a figure to die for. I'm afraid she attracted the attention of lots of men."

"Any particular men?" Moore said.

"We have very strict rules about fraternization between the staff and the students. It's a big no-no. But some of the teachers are more or less the same age as the students, so it's very hard to police. Now, I'm not going to say any more about it. That's your job, Detective," O'Sullivan said as they arrived at the office door.

Moore decided not to share her information about Peter Ledwidge with the school. Not for now, in any case.

When O'Sullivan had opened the office door, and was about to go in leaving Moore in the corridor with the files, Moore said, "Janet, we need to speak to two of Alicia's friends. Let me see," – she consulted her notebook – "yes, here we are, Maria Gomez and Isabella Hernandez. Where would we find them?"

"You'd better come in and let me look up their timetable, Sergeant."

Moore followed the woman into her office. The room was in immaculate order, if rather full of stuff, but everything seemed to be well organized. Her desk was clear, except for a small pile of post that Moore assumed had been delivered that morning, a phone, a PC screen, keyboard and mouse and a microphone on a stand that was connected to a box on a shelf behind the desk with glowing LED lights. O'Sullivan got busy consulting her computer, and after a moment or two navigating with the mouse, looked up.

"Yes, here we are. They should be just finishing in room G4. If you like I can put a call out on the tannoy?"

"Yes, would you, please. And is there somewhere we could talk to them in private for a few minutes?"

"Yes, of course. You can use my office here. I need a cup of coffee anyway."

Janet O'Sullivan pressed the red button on the stem of the microphone and spoke into it.

"Maria Gomez and Isabella Hernandez to the office please." And then she repeated the summons.

Moore could hear the message echoing through the corridors, and was surprised how clear it was.

Chapter Fourteen

"Dónal, it's Amy. Any news on the missing Spanish woman?" Sutton said.

"No, not a whisper. What are you up to?"

"We're at the school. The boss wants someone to start digging into the background of the woman who runs the place, a Mrs Walker, and anything that pops up about the school too. Are you mad busy?"

"Not too bad. The Ortez girl's parents are coming over later. They want to see their daughter, and then they want to talk to us. I'm not looking forward to that very much," Lawler said.

"Can't you get the inspector to handle that?"

"Not likely. He's in a really weird humour for some reason or other. I'm staying well out of his way."

"Ha! Good idea. Sergeant Moore wants us to escalate the missing girl thing too. She has a bad feeling about it, and to be honest, so do I."

"Right, I'll get on it. Oh, and you can tell the boss that I've started doing the background check on Ledwidge she asked for. Nothing of interest so far, but it's early days."

"Great. OK. Chat later." Sutton went back into the school to wait for Fiona Moore. As she waited, she strolled along the corridors and scanned the noticeboards which were covered in advertisements of one kind or another. There were some handwritten postcards offering accommodation. Others, where additional students were required to share existing apartments, giving details of the rent and associated costs, and several more professional-looking posters for various venues around the town. One nightclub in particular seemed to dominate the space. Club Ozone offered a variety of themed entertainment. Of particular interest was 'Spanish Night' which they featured every Thursday and held out the promise of tapas and sangria as well as the very latest in European sounds. There was no phone number on the posters, but the club had a website, and Amy Sutton made a note of it in her pocketbook.

Moore came out of the office and re-joined her colleague.

"OK, Sarge?" Sutton said.

"Yes, fine. Let's wait here till the other two students arrive. Ms O'Sullivan says we can use her office to talk to them. Any news from the station?"

"No, not a thing. I spoke to Dónal. He just said the inspector is in a bit of a grumpy mood."

"Yes, I know. I'm sure you are aware there has been a complaint made against him," Moore said.

"Yes, I did hear something about that," Sutton said.

"I don't suppose anyone has any idea who made the complaint."

"No, I didn't hear anything about that. I doubt if it's anyone we know. We're a pretty loyal bunch, us lot, don't you think?"

"Hmm... I suppose, but someone did it, and it looks as if it is being taken seriously too," Moore said.

"Really? What will happen?"

"I don't know, Amy, but it could be quite awkward for him. Anyway, here are our two students by the look of things."

Two young women who looked to be something like twenty years old were heading down the corridor chattering and giggling in Spanish. They arrived at the office door and knocked, and when Janet O'Sullivan opened the door, she invited them in. Moore and Sutton followed, and introductions were made.

When they were all seated and O'Sullivan had left in search of refreshment, Moore addressed the two students.

"Thank you for coming to the office, ladies. We understand you are both friends of Alicia Navarro, is that right?"

The woman whom they now knew to be Isabella Hernandez answered.

"Yes, we are all friends. Why do you ask?"

"I see. Does Alicia have a regular boyfriend?" Sutton asked.

The two girls looked at each other and giggled for a second.

Isabella replied, "More than one."

Moore looked at Sutton and then back to the student.

"Can you explain, please, Isabella?"

"Alicia is very popular with the boys. Sometimes it seems she is trying to be with as many Irishmen as she can before she goes home to Spain. But maybe we should not have said anything. It's personal."

"Isabella, I'm not sure if you have heard, but we think Alicia may have gone missing. She is not at her bedsit in Capel Street, and Mr Ledwidge called us to say he was concerned. He hasn't been able to contact her. Do you have any idea where she might be?"

The two Spanish students looked at each other with serious faces, all the giddiness now gone from them.

"No, not at all. Is she all right?" Maria Gomez said.

"We hope so, but after what happened to Gabriella, we don't want to take any chances. Do you know the names of any of the men Alicia was seeing, apart from Mr Ledwidge?" Moore asked.

"No. She spoke of a Paul and a guy called Michael sometimes, but we don't know where they are from or anything else about them," Isabella said.

"You never met these men when you were out with Alicia at a club or in a bar?" Sutton said.

"No. Sorry," Maria said.

"Where did Alicia meet these men, at first, I mean?" Moore said.

"I think in Ozone. It's a club quite close. She went there quite a lot, especially on Thursday when they do a sort of Spanish night," Isabella said.

"And did you ever go with her to Ozone?" Sutton said.

"Yes, but not every week. We have a class here on Thursday evening sometimes, so by the time that is finished and we get our food, we are too tired to go to the club."

Moore looked at Sutton and they exchanged slight nods.

"OK. Thank you both for talking to us. If you hear from Alicia, please let us know immediately, and ask her to get in touch with one of us. Here's my card." Moore gave both of them a card each with her contact details.

* * *

When Moore and Sutton got back to Sutton's car, Amy asked Moore about her own vehicle.

"When will your car be back from the menders, boss?"

"They said they'd have it later on today for me. I hope they've done a decent job on it. I know it's not exactly a Rolls Royce, but I'm attached to it all the same," Moore said.

"Was there much damage?"

"Nine hundred and fifty euro's worth, according to the estimate. But I think the landlord is going to cover it from his insurance. That's what he said in any case."

"Cripes! He must have done a right old number on it. Any idea who it was that did it over?"

"No. None. But if I catch the little scumbag, he'll be sorry he was ever born! Look, there's no point in trying Ozone at this time of day, they won't be open for ages yet. Let's head back to the station and see what's turned up, if anything," Moore said.

Chapter Fifteen

Dónal Lawler was trying to find out about Gabriella Ortez's bank card. It was less than straightforward. He had got as far as finding out that she used a Revolut card, and Lawler knew that the issuer was regulated in Lithuania, but they had representation in the UK, and one or two of the Irish banks, somewhat reluctantly, had arrangements with them too. Just when he thought he might be getting somewhere with his investigations, Aidan Burke came out of his office.

"C'mon, Dónal, leave that. We need to go."

Lawler locked his PC screen, grabbed his jacket and tried to catch up with his boss who was already halfway to the car park.

"What's the rush, boss?" he said as they approached Burke's car.

"I've had a call from Crumlin. They think there's a body in the grass up by the canal, somewhere near the Sally's Bridge. Can you get on the blower to Moore and see where the hell she is? Get her to meet us up there. It's just off Lullymore Terrace."

When they were underway, Lawler said, "That's your neck of the woods, isn't it, boss?"

"Well, sort of. I'm not actually near the canal, but I know the area all the same. Jesus! The traffic is brutal," Burke said. He manoeuvred deftly between lines of stationery vehicles with the blue lights and sirens, but it always frustrated him when other drivers didn't seem to share the urgency of his mission.

"Who found the body, boss?" Lawler said.

"The usual. A dog walker. Seems she's pretty distressed, but they are keeping her there till we arrive."

"OK. Yeah, I guess that might put you off your lunch. Oh, shit!"

"What?" Burke said.

"Aren't the Ortez parents coming in this afternoon?"

"Yes, you're right. I think Sutton is with Sergeant Moore. When we get there, I'll send her back into town to deal with them."

Burke blasted his car horn to add to the cacophony his vehicle was already making to try and clear a large white van out of the way. The van pulled in a little, and Burke got a two-fingered salute for his trouble as they passed it out.

* * *

When they arrived at Lullymore Terrace, Burke abandoned his car at the top of the narrow street, just in front of the blue-and-white tape that had been erected by the uniformed Gardaí who were attending the scene. Lullymore Terrace was a long row of single-storey, terraced, red-brick-fronted houses that faced the verge of the canal, although their view of the water was obscured by tall grasses, weeds and bushes that had taken root in the fertile soil. Dublin City Council had stopped trimming the banks some time ago in the interests of allowing wild flowers to take over, but Burke thought it was probably more about saving money than any altruistic attempt to assist Mother Nature.

The Garda protecting the scene took a note of Burke and Lawler's names, and gestured for them to pass under the tape. They moved together towards the grassy bank where they could see white-suited forensic officers already at work. Aileen Brophy was on her hunkers delicately examining what was clearly the body of a young woman.

"Afternoon, Aileen. What have we got?" Burke said.

"Hello, Aidan. I can't be one hundred percent certain yet, but I think it's the body of a young Spanish woman. At least, that's what it looks like from her clothes."

"Any ID?"

"Not per se, no. It looks like all her personal stuff has been taken. No purse, handbag, phone or anything, just a few tissues in her jeans pocket, and a few euro in change."

"How long has she been here?" Lawler said.

"Let's see. Given the weather, and the locale, I'd say probably since late last night," Brophy said.

"Did she die here?" Burke said.

"Yes, almost certainly. And before you ask, she was strangled. Manual strangulation I'd wager, and she's been knocked about a good bit too. I'll know more when we get her back to town, but there is a cut just above her left eye, and I think she may have been punched a few times in the stomach. Oh, and her shoes are missing."

"Lovely. Dónal, why don't you take a few uniforms and start the house-to-house. And see if there's any CCTV anywhere that could give us something. There may be a camera up at the bridge for traffic monitoring."

As Dónal Lawler was walking away to start the well-practiced procedure as instructed, Moore and Sutton arrived.

"Hello, boss. What's the story?" Moore said.

"Aileen says she thinks the woman is Spanish, judging by her clothes. But there's no proper ID on her, and all her stuff is gone."

"In the canal, maybe?" Moore said.

"Yes, maybe. Can you get the sub-aqua team out again? Oh, and, Amy, I need you to get back into town to meet Gabriella Ortez's parents. They should be arriving soon. If they are up to it, ask if they know anything about who their daughter was friendly with here in Dublin, and of course get a formal identity on the girl. I'll give Sergeant Moore a lift back to town in a while," Burke said.

Burke turned to Moore. "Can you get a proper search of this area organised for us? Anything could have been discarded in the long grass and reeds. I'm going to talk to the woman who found the body."

"Right, boss."

* * *

Mrs Cynthia O'Gorman was a stoutish woman, probably in her early seventies. She was dressed in a warm camel coat, and was accompanied by a small, beige dog whom she kept on a colourful lead. She was sitting on the wall close to where the body had been found, with a female Garda stranding close by her. When Burke approached, the female officer introduced him, and he sat on the wall beside the woman so as not to intimidate her.

"Thank you for waiting, Mrs O'Gorman. This must be very distressing for you. May I ask what time it was when you came across the body?" Burke said.

"It must have been around eleven-thirty. I had been to the shops up across the bridge getting a few bits and pieces, and was walking back on the path just beside the water. Nemo likes to have a good sniff around," she said, gesturing towards the little pet.

"He started straining on the leash, which is not like him at all, so I went to investigate, and there she was. This is terrible, officer, this is such a quiet place normally."

"Did you touch anything, Mrs O'Gorman?" Burke said.

"No, of course not. What do you take me for?"

"Which house do you live in, Mrs O'Gorman?"

"Number twelve. It's further along. Why?"

Burke realised that the woman he was dealing with was very competent, and not a bit doddery.

"Tell me about last night. Did you hear or see anything out of the ordinary?"

"No, nothing at all. I was watching TV in the front room with Nemo. My programme finished at ten. Then I watched the news headlines, got myself a hot drink at about quarter past, and went to bed shortly before eleven. But I didn't see or hear anything unusual though."

Burke tried not to let his frustration show.

"So, is there anything else you can tell me, Mrs O'Gorman?"

"Yes, there is, Inspector. You see that old car down near the end of the terrace, outside number 24?"

Burke glanced down the road and spotted a rather beaten-up-looking Hyundai parked in an untidy manner near the end of the terrace.

"Do you mean the old Hyundai?"

"Yes. That car doesn't belong here. Mr Byrne who lives there doesn't have a car, and that one isn't owned by anyone else on the road," O'Gorman said.

"Have you any idea when it arrived?"

"Overnight, I think. It wasn't there yesterday, but I saw it this morning."

"Did you see who brought it here, or anyone getting out of it?"

"No, Inspector, I didn't. But I know all the cars that park along here, and that's not one of them."

"Right, Mrs O'Gorman, thanks very much for your help. Are you feeling OK now?"

"Yes. I'm fine thank you, Inspector. Can I go now? I'm getting cold."

"Yes, of course. Thanks again."

Burke walked back up to where the forensic officers were still working all around where the woman's body had been found. He collared one of the team.

"Can you get to the old Hyundai that's parked badly down at the end of the road. One of the neighbours said it doesn't belong here. See if it's locked, and if not have a look inside. Oh, and check the reg with the database as well. It may have been stolen."

"OK, sir, I'm on it."

Chapter Sixteen

Burke and Moore both decided to go along to the post-mortem on the latest victim which Aileen Brophy had said she would start at three o'clock.

When they arrived at the mortuary, Brophy was already togged out in her work clothes. The girl was laid out on the gurney, naked, except for a plain white opaque cloth covering her dignity.

"Ah, two for the price of one," Brophy said in an uncharacteristically glib manner.

Burke and Moore just grunted an acknowledgement.

"Right. Let's get started then."

Brophy began by walking around the body, carefully examining the woman's skin, paying particular attention to her head and neck. She took a magnifying glass from her assistant, and scrutinized the wounds that were apparent on the woman's throat, before standing up and declaring, "Definite manual strangulation. But this one put up a fight. If I'm not mistaken, chummy may have some scratches on his face, and we should be able to get skin samples from under her fingernails."

Brophy lifted one of the woman's limp arms and examined her hand carefully.

"Yes, there's definitely biological material here, and it looks as if she pulled a few hairs out of her assailant's head too. They are still in her fist. With any luck we'll be able to get a DNA sample for you."

"How soon could we expect that, Dr Brophy?" Burke said.

"If I expedite it with the lab, I might have it back tomorrow."

"Thanks, yes please," Burke said.

Brophy continued her examination of the body, turning her attention to the corpse's exposed legs and feet.

"There's some mud and grass on her left foot. Looks like she lost a shoe in the struggle. You'll probably find that at the scene."

"Any sign of sexual interference, Doctor?"

"Let me see." Brophy removed the cloth from the woman's groin area and continued her examination.

"There's no bruising in this area, and no residue of any kind, so I'd say no to rape or forced sex in any case. But I think there are what looks like splashes of dried semen on her lower leg. So, there was a sexual dimension to the attack for sure, I'll know more when I've had a good look inside."

Brophy nodded to her assistant who had been standing off with a large rectangular stainless-steel tray covered in gruesome instruments. He moved in closer to his boss to enable her to start cutting up the hapless victim.

"I'll just go and have a chat with Ruth, boss," Moore said, keen to escape the gorier part of the process. She walked away to the back room in the path lab where Ruth was busy examining specimens under one of her microscopes.

"Hi, Ruth. Anything interesting among the woman's clothes?" Moore said.

"Hi, Fiona. Yes, there is as it happens. She had an inside pocket in her jeans. I've seen these once or twice before. It's for keeping your ID card, or a few well-folded euro notes away from pickpockets."

"Wow! I never heard of that before. Find anything in it?"

"Yes. A bank card," Ruth said. She held up a small red card showing it to Moore.

"Issued by Banco Santander in Alicante last year, and valid till the end of next year. It's in the name of Martina Alicia Navarro."

"Oh, gosh. Well, that more or less confirms the woman's identity for us in any case. Damn! What's with this guy going after all these Spanish women, for God's sake?"

"Who knows? Maybe he got a bad paella when he was on holiday in Benidorm or something," Ruth said.

"But look, I'd better get back and tell the boss. Can you be sure to expedite the DNA tests for us? Chummy may be known to us."

"Yes, of course. I'll let you know the minute we get anything."

Moore re-joined her boss, trying not to look too closely at the process of removing Alicia's organs that Brophy was getting on with.

"Hi, boss. Well, we now know who she is in any case. Ruth confirmed her name as Martina Alicia Navarro. It was on a bank card hidden in her jeans."

"Hmm... OK, well I'll finish up here with the good doctor. I want you to go around to The World of English and ask them to put in safety measures for their female students. You know the drill."

"Right, boss. See you back at the nick later then."

"Yeah, see you."

* * *

Moore collected a squad car from the Garda station car park, which as luck would have it was only a stone's throw from the City Morgue where Dr Brophy and her team did their work. She drove out briskly to Nottingham Street where once again the pavement outside The World of English was thronged with students of various nationalities.

Moore parked in a handy loading bay and went into the building.

"Hello again, Karla. I'd like to see Mrs Walker, please," Moore said to the receptionist.

"Hello, Sergeant. I'll see if she is available." Karla reached for the phone and dialled a two-digit number. Moore couldn't hear the exchange between the two women, but after a few moments, Karla hung up and said, "I'm sorry, Sergeant, Mrs Walker is tied up at the moment. She asked if you could make an appointment, maybe for tomorrow."

"Look, Karla, your female students are being bumped off one after another here. If Mrs Walker doesn't think that's important enough to see me, then perhaps we should just close the place down for a few weeks while we get to the bottom of it. Give it one more try for me, and if that doesn't work, consider the school closed, OK?"

Karla said nothing but went back to the relative sanctuary of the phone. She spoke in muted tones for a brief minute.

"Mrs Walker says she will see you. Do you know where her office is?" Karla said rather unhelpfully.

"I'll find it, don't worry," Moore said rather caustically.

When she reached the office door with 'Mrs E Walker, Principal' engraved upon it, Moore knocked and went straight in. Walker looked up from her desk, surprised that Moore had not waited to be invited to enter.

"Really, Sergeant, this is most inconvenient. I was in the middle of something very important. I didn't wish to be disturbed."

"And what may I ask were you in the middle of, Mrs Walker?" Moore said, taking a seat in front of the woman's desk.

"I think that's my business, Sergeant, don't you?"

"Whatever."

"So, what is it that is so important that it couldn't wait?"

Moore told Walker that another one of their female Spanish students had been murdered and her body found up along the canal.

"Well, of course, I'm very sorry to hear that, Sergeant, but as I said before, what they get up to in their own time is really not anything to do with me or the school. I'm sure you understand."

Moore could barely believe what she was hearing.

"No, Mrs Walker, I don't understand. I don't understand at all. It's clear to me and my team that your school is the common thread that links these killings. It's got to be more than a coincidence that both of the dead women were attending here, don't you think?"

"What exactly are you implying, Sergeant?"

Moore realised she was unlikely to get anywhere using the confrontational approach, so she changed tack.

"Mrs Walker, I've been investigating murders for several years now, and I'm pretty good at it, as is Inspector Burke. My experience tells me that there is very rarely, in fact almost never, any coincidences in this business. Or to put it another way, if it looks like a duck, and it quacks like a duck, then the chances are…"

"So, you think there is a connection to the school then?"

"Yes, though what I have no idea as yet. But before we get into that, I want you to address the female cohort here and give them advice on how to stay safe. I want them going around in pairs or bigger groups. No one-to-one dating for the moment. No getting into strangers' cars. No out alone at night, and stay away from both of the canals. Can you do that?" Moore said.

"Won't that be likely to cause panic among the girls, Sergeant?"

"I'd prefer a little fear than more dead bodies, Mrs Walker. And I'm still waiting for a detailed list of all your male students, with photos, home addresses and any other information you may hold on them, and the same for any male teachers you employ. And I'd like another word with Gomez and Hernandez before I leave if you could have them called to the office."

Mrs Walker finally appeared to be taking the matter seriously. She summoned Janet O'Sullivan and asked her to accompany Moore while they went and rooted out the two Spaniards.

"While you're doing that, I'll prepare a handbill with your suggestions on it and have it distributed to all the young women here," Walker said.

"Thanks."

Moore got up and went out with Janet O'Sullivan to find Maria Gomez and Isabella Hernandez.

Chapter Seventeen

The two young women arrived together in Janet O'Sullivan's office a few minutes later.

"Thanks, Janet," Moore said. "Come in, take a seat, girls."

The two sat down looking a little apprehensive.

"Thanks. Listen, folks, I'm afraid I have some bad news for the two of you," Moore said. She waited a moment before continuing, giving the young women some time to prepare themselves for what was to come. She then continued.

"The body of a young woman has been found at the side of the canal up near Dolphin's Barn. We believe it may be that of Alicia Navarro, I'm terribly sorry."

The two Spaniards looked briefly at each other before starting to cry. Maria sobbed loudly, and Janet O'Sullivan provided tissues to both of them, while Isabella wept silently, with big tears rolling down her cheeks. Moore gave them several minutes to digest the awful news before continuing.

"I'm sorry, Maria, Isabella, but we need to ask a few questions, if you are up to it?"

The two women nodded.

"May I ask if you know anything about Alicia's movements last night? Was she planning to meet anyone, or go anywhere that you know of?"

"I don't know. She often met with Peter Ledwidge after all the classes here had finished about nine o'clock, but I don't know if that was what she had planned for last night," Maria said.

"When did you last see Alicia?"

"I told you before. The day before yesterday. She was at class as usual. She left at about five like we all did. I assumed she was going home," Isabella said.

"She said nothing about meeting anyone, or going somewhere different?" Moore said.

"No, nothing like that," Isabella said.

"Was she in good form, cheerful, or did she seem worried by anything?"

"Alicia was always happy, Sergeant, always smiling and joking with everyone," Maria said, starting to cry again in earnest.

"When were you last out with Alicia?" Moore said looking from one to the other.

"Thursday last week. We all went to Ozone for their Spanish night. We skipped the evening class. Alicia was with us then," Isabella said.

"Did you see her with anyone that night?"

Maria looked at Isabella.

"Yes. At one point she was talking to a boy. They seemed to be having a disagreement about something, but afterwards, she wouldn't talk about it. When I asked her what it was, she laughed it off. She said it was nothing," Maria said.

"What did this boy look like?"

"Just ordinary. I didn't pay much attention, and it was quite dark in the club," Isabella said.

"And did Alicia say she was going to meet this man at any stage?"

"No, she didn't refer to it at all. Oh my God, do you think he was the killer?" Maria Gomez said.

"We don't know, I'm afraid. It's just the start of the investigation. But listen, this is the second Spanish woman to lose her life who was attending this college. I don't want to scare you, but you need to take some precautions. You should be very careful especially at night. Don't ever get into a stranger's car on your own, and it would be better if you could go around in twos until we get this sorted out. If you encounter any suspicious behaviour at all, call the police immediately. Is that clear?"

The two women looked at each other again.

"Yes, it's clear, officer," Isabella said.

Moore decided that there was not much more she could do at the college. She hoped Mrs Walker was taking her advice seriously, and would comply with her instructions. She thanked Gomez, Hernandez and Janet O'Sullivan and left to go back to the station.

* * *

Back at Store Street there was lots happening. Amy Sutton had met with Gabriella Ortez's parents, and was sitting sombrely at her desk. Moore walked over.

"Everything all right, Amy?"

"Not really, boss. Mr and Mrs Ortez have been. God, it was awful. They were terribly upset. Gabriella was their only child, and they had high hopes for her. She was quite clever it seems, and they had expectations that she would take over her father's business in due course."

Moore didn't really want to know what the Ortez family business was, but she recognised that her colleague needed to talk, so she asked, "And what business is Mr Ortez in?"

"He has a factory that manufactures leather goods – bags, shoes and some clothing. Apparently, they export all over Europe. It's a pretty big operation it seems. Mrs Ortez wanted to know if these kinds of crimes were common in Ireland. I didn't have the heart to tell her that we possibly had another one on our books," Sutton said.

"Are they staying over in Dublin?"

"Yes, just for the night. They have to get back to Madrid tomorrow. There are some important business meetings arranged that can't be delayed."

"OK. Well, thanks anyway, Amy. I'm sorry if that was upsetting for you. Any other news?" Moore said.

"Oh, yes, I nearly forgot. Forensics were on. They've retrieved records from Gabriella's phone. They are sending over the details shortly. And they lifted the car up at the other site and are bringing it back in. Apparently, it was right out of fuel. How did you get on at the school?"

"We met Alicia's friends, but they weren't much help if truth were told. Someone needs to go and visit the nightclub they all frequent as soon as it opens just in case they might have CCTV. Or maybe some of the staff will remember something. Any sign of the boss?" Moore said.

"I think he's in his office," Sutton said.

"Thanks."

Moore went in search of Burke, who, as Sutton had said, was in his office.

"Hello, boss. What's the story?"

"Hi, Fiona. I'm just back from the second murder scene. Jesus, we need to get a handle on this lot pronto before there's another one. Can you set up a briefing for later, say five o'clock? Get everyone in, and see if Keith could come across from forensics as well. Has Dónal hacked into her PC yet?" Burke said.

"I'm not sure. I'll go and ask him if you like."

"Yes, please. Anything useful from the school?"

"No, sorry. But I did get a rather uneasy feeling about the principal, a Mrs Walker. She didn't seem to be as upset as I would have expected."

"Yes, but I hardly see her as a murderer!"

Chapter Eighteen

The team came together at five o'clock as Burke had requested.

"OK, everyone, settle down. Let's go around the room and see what we've got. Dónal, you first."

"Thanks, boss. Well, I've been able to get into Gabriella's PC now. It booted up fine after it thawed out. There was a password, but I guessed it after a few attempts. Her email is interesting. She's been exchanging messages with someone called Alfonso. The messages are very cryptic." Lawler handed out a few pages of print-out to each of the other members of the team.

Alfonso had sent a single word message to Gabriella a week before she died. '*Llegado?*' it said. She had replied with another short message, '*Todavía no*,' to which Alfonso had responded, '*Mañana'*.

"What does all this mean, Dónal? My Spanish only stretches to *cerveza* and *paella*," Burke said.

"In the first message Alfonso is asking if it has arrived, whatever 'it' is. She says not yet, and he says tomorrow. Two days later, Gabriella sends another message saying, 'It's here', and he replies, 'Terrific'. That's it. End of story."

"Have you traced the IP address of Alfonso?" Moore said.

"No dice. He's using a VPN. That's a Virtual Private Network to you and me. It means the location of the sender is anonymised. He could be anywhere in the world," Lawler said.

"Fantastic!" Moore said.

Keith put up his hand.

"We may have had a bit more luck with her phone, sir," he said.

"OK, do tell, Keith."

"We've been able to construct a timeline from the calls she made and received over the last month or so. It was pretty tricky because lots of them were just quick messages to her mates arranging to meet here and there and slagging off some of the young men in the college. But there is a thread running through it with someone in the Netherlands. No name, but again, a few cryptic messages. I have them here," he said.

He too handed out a few pages of A4 paper with the transcript of the calls he had been talking about. The group studied them.

"This looks like it's to do with money, boss," Moore said. "There are what appear to me cash amounts, some of them quite large too."

"Have we had any luck with her bank account?" Burke said.

"No, sir. If you recall, her account is with Revolut, and they won't part with any information. It doesn't help that they are in Lithuania, but they are hiding behind all that GDPR crap. They won't tell me anything."

"For fuck's sake, can we get a warrant or something? If this is all about money, we need that information. And what about the number we found in her clothing? Have we traced that yet?" Burke said.

"No, sir. Not yet. We've been kind of busy," Moore said.

"I know, I know, but let's get on with it. What about the background checks on the woman from the school and the teachers and students?" Burke said.

"We're still looking into them all, boss, but nothing startling has come up so far. And there's nothing from the CCTV either, I'm afraid," Moore said.

"Yeah, let's shake it all up a bit. Now, Keith, have you anything else for us?" Burke said.

"Not yet, sir, but they're doing the PM on the second victim at the moment, and we have the car back here now too, so there may be something later on."

"Have we any of her personal belongings yet?" Moore said.

"No, Sarge, but they are still searching the site where she was found."

"OK. Someone needs to get back down to Capel Street and do a proper search of her place," Moore said.

"Right, boss. I'll get on it as soon as we're finished here," Sutton said.

"I need someone to stay on this tonight. I want the results of the PM as soon as they are finished, and anything else that comes to light. Have we warned the other female students at the college to be careful?" Burke said.

"Yes, sir. The school has issued a handbill, and we've told Walker to tell them all to be extra careful," Moore said.

"Right. Dónal, will you co-ordinate things here while Amy is dealing with Ledwidge. Sergeant, you and I are going clubbing!" Burke said.

* * *

It was just after seven when Burke and Moore arrived at Ozone, having stopped along the way for some sustenance. The club was in a lane behind Bachelor's Walk along the Liffey known as North Lotts. It got its strange name from a developer called Jonathan Amory who purchased a tranche of land there in the seventeenth century, and having drained it, and done some preparations, sold it off in parcels or lots, giving the place its title. It was a narrow street with a variety of rather seedy premises along its length, many of which were daubed with what was romantically called street art, but to Burke and Moore just looked like graffiti.

Ozone was about halfway along the lane. Its exterior was mostly painted black, but the street artists had been at it and added abstract shapes in gaudy shades of yellow, orange and green. There was a pink neon sign over the door that was illuminated, and the detectives found the door open and unmanned. They went in.

The inside of the club was dark and quite dingy. There was a smell of stale beer that was vying with some ghastly floral air freshener for dominance in the somewhat fetid atmosphere. Cleaners, dressed in black jeans and black T-shirts were mopping the floor and dusting the rather decrepit furniture. All along the back wall of the place a long bar that was better illuminated than the rest of the joint displayed taps for more than a dozen draught concoctions, and at the back there were bottles and bottles of well-known, and some not so well-known, spirits. Burke spotted a sturdy mesh grid rolled away in a box section above the counter which presumably could be lowered rapidly to protect the staff if a serious fracas broke out on the dance floor.

Behind the bar, a middle-aged man with long greasy grey hair was busy preparing for the night ahead. He looked up as Burke and Moore approached.

"Sorry, we're not open yet. Come back after ten," he said, knowing full well that they were not patrons, but feeling the need to dispense with the visitors as quickly as he could.

"We haven't come here to party, mate. Are you in charge?" Burke said. He held up his warrant card for the man to inspect, which was quite unnecessary as it was obvious from the outset that Burke was a Garda.

The man stopped what he was doing, and looked Burke in the eye. "I am."

"What's your name, sir?" Moore said.

"Larry." He was obviously a man of few words.

"Larry what?" Moore said.

"Just Larry. What do you want?"

"We are making enquiries about some of the students who were in last Thursday. Is that when you have your Spanish night?" Burke said.

"Hmph. Bloody noisy lot. And if I hear that fucking Macarena one more time, I'll ban the bloody lot of them," Larry said.

"I presume they pay an entrance fee and buy lots of overpriced drinks when they are here?" Moore said.

Larry just shrugged.

"Have you any CCTV on the premises, Larry?"

"You must be joking! With what goes on in here you wouldn't want it on camera, and that's all I'm saying."

"And what would that be, Larry?" Burke said.

"Ah, you know what young people get up to these days."

"Nothing illegal, I presume?" Burke said.

Larry just shrugged again.

"So, is there any point in asking you about some of the Spanish students then?" Moore said.

"None at all, Guard."

"What about outside. Any CCTV out there?" Burke said.

"I dunno. Why don't you go and have a look?"

Burke glanced at Moore who sensed that his patience was being sorely tried.

"I'll tell you what, Larry. Why don't we just close this place down for a week or so while we get Revenue and Customs in here to go through all your VAT receipts and your drink stocks. And I'll need a full list of your membership as well, and now would be good."

"Fuck you," Larry muttered.

"Sorry, what was that?" Burke said. He moved in closer to the bar.

Larry didn't respond.

Burke got up close and personal to the barman.

"Now listen here, you prick. I'm just that far away from arresting you for obstruction in a murder enquiry," he said. He held his finger and thumb up a centimetre apart in front of Larry's face. "If you don't start co-operating, Revenue will be the least of your worries."

Burke leaned across the bar and took up an almost full bottle of vodka and dropped it on the hard floor where it smashed into several pieces before repeating the exercise with a bottle of whiskey.

"Oops! You'd better get that lot cleaned up before someone gets hurt," Burke said.

Larry looked disbelievingly at the detective.

Burke took a photo of Gabriella Ortez out of his pocket and showed it to Larry.

"Did you see this woman in here last Thursday?"

Larry had apparently got the message.

"Look, mate. On Thursdays this place is jammed with loads of young noisy Spanish students. They're dancing, drinking, snogging and maybe more, and all I can do is keep up with the demand for drink at the bar, and that's me and three other barmen. We don't have a chance to notice anyone in particular. I'm sorry I can't help you, but that's just the way it is."

Burke looked at Moore and nodded towards the door.

"We may be back," he said.

They both turned around and left the club. Outside, they looked up and down the street, but could see no evidence of CCTV cameras on any of the buildings, which they thought a bit odd.

"It doesn't look as if there's any CCTV here. Maybe we could get Dublin City Council to put some up. They could say it is for traffic control if anyone is asking. Can you look into it for me?"

"OK, boss. Let's get back to the station."

Chapter Nineteen

It was after eight when they got back to Store Street. Moore checked her emails, and found that a preliminary report had been sent across by Aileen Brophy from the post-mortem on Alicia Navarro. She sent the email to the printer which started whirring and clicking obligingly. She took the two pages from the printer and went into Burke's office.

"What have you there?" Burke said.

"It's the prelim from the Navarro post-mortem."

"Oh. Anything interesting?"

"Hmm, let me see. Cause of death, manual strangulation. Time of death, between 10:00 p.m. and 1:00 a.m. the night before she was found. Toxicology to be advised, results awaited. Other observations, skin particles removed from under the victim's fingernails. That's been sent for DNA analysis, again results awaited. No evidence of sexual interference. That's about it, boss."

"Well, that's something, I guess. Maybe we'll know more in a day or two. Anything further back from forensics on the car?"

"No, not yet. I'll chase it up tomorrow," Moore said.

"OK. Have we notified the Spanish Embassy about the second victim?"

"I'm not sure. Dónal has gone home. I'll check with him in the morning. Will there be anything else tonight, boss?"

"No. We're done. You get off. See you in the morning. Oh, by the way, did you get your car back?" Burke said.

"Yes. They left it here during the afternoon. I haven't seen it yet, but Danny says it looks as good as new."

"OK, cool. See you tomorrow then."

"Yeah, goodnight."

* * *

Moore gathered her things and went downstairs where she got the keys of her car from the desk sergeant. The car was parked in the car park, and from what Moore could see, they had done a nice job on it. The windscreen was cleaner than it had ever been before, and the door mirrors gleamed with reflections from the overhead lights in the car park. The doors too had been repainted, and Moore felt good about it as she got in and started the engine.

When she was halfway home, her phone, which she had left on the front passenger's seat with her handbag, beeped. Moore recognised the sound as that of an incoming WhatsApp message. She didn't stop to see who it was from, but when she got into the car park, she looked at the message.

Glad your car is OK again. Sorry!

A chill ran through her.

She removed a small container of pepper spray from the glove compartment, collected her handbag and jacket, and got out of the car. She looked around the car park, but could see no one, although there were plenty of places someone could be hiding behind pillars or down behind other vehicles. She walked briskly to the small grey door that led into the stairwell, glancing all around her as she went, but it appeared that she was on her own. Once she got inside her apartment, she started breathing properly again. She examined the phone and made a note of the number that had sent the WhatsApp message. It wasn't already in her contact list, so she determined to follow that up with the technical boys tomorrow.

* * *

The following morning Burke arrived in the car park of Store Street Garda station at exactly the same time as his boss, Superintendent Jerome Heffernan. As Burke stepped out of his vehicle, he greeted the senior man, "Good morning, sir."

"Ah, hello, Aidan. I'm glad I ran into you. I need a word."

Heffernan stood still where he was, making it clear to Burke that their tête-à-tête would be outdoors where no one could overhear.

"I just wanted to update you about that complaint."

"Yes, thanks, what's the story?" Burke said.

"It's all gone quiet for now, though that doesn't mean it's gone away, Aidan. But with these Spanish murders going on, I'm not having one of my senior officers transferred just at the moment. I can't afford that, so you're safe for now."

"That's great news, sir. Thank you."

"Don't thank me yet. It could still blow up in our faces, believe me. But the longer it goes on, the more likely it is to be dropped. That is unless yer one starts telling fancy tales when she gets to court. She's appealing her sentence, you know?"

"No, I didn't know that. Obviously, I haven't been in touch with anyone over it."

"Obviously. Anyway, are you making any progress on the Spanish killings?" Heffernan said. He moved towards the station entrance.

"Some, sir, but it's early days yet."

"This is bad news Aidan. I've already had a call from the mayor saying that the TEFL business is vital to the economy of the city, and if the Spanish stop coming it will mean several of the schools will have to close."

"I take it he didn't have any suggestions as to who might be behind the murders then?" Burke said.

"That would be your job, Aidan. I'd better let you get on with it. Keep me posted with any positive developments, won't you?" Heffernan said.

"Yes, of course, sir."

On the way up the stairs to his office, Burke's mood was much improved following the chat with his boss.

* * *

When Burke reached his office, he had barely sat down when Dónal Lawler appeared at the door.

"Have you got a minute, sir?" Lawler said.

"Yes, of course, Dónal, come in. Tell you what, before we start, why don't you slip across the road and get us all a nice hot coffee and a box of those doughnuts. See if anyone outside want some too," Burke said. He handed Lawler a €20 note.

"OK, boss. That's very generous of you. I'll be back in a few minutes."

Lawler wondered what had got into the man. While he wasn't considered mean – he always stood his round in the pub willingly – this was quite out of character. In any case, Lawler picked up orders from Moore and Sutton and went out to get the goodies. He was back in less than ten minutes and having left coffees and doughnuts for his colleagues, he went back into Burke's office.

"Great, Dónal, thanks. Now what's on your mind?" Burke said.

"I've had forensics on about the car, sir. It's very odd. There are loads of prints all over the steering wheel and the door handles, and they think they will be able to get

DNA off it too. It looks as if there was no attempt to wipe it down."

"That's odd. Are we sure it's connected to the girl's murder? Maybe it was just dumped there by some joyriders or something."

"We'll know later today, sir. There was a spent tissue found in the passenger's footwell, and that definitely will have some DNA on it. If it matches the victims, then bingo!"

"Excellent. But before all that comes through, there's a little job I want you to do for me."

"OK. What's that, sir?"

"I'd like you to go back out to Ranelagh, to where Gabriella Ortez lived. I want you to empty out the recycling bin and look for any packaging that you can find addressed to her. According to her emails, she received something, and it's just possible the packaging is still there. But you need to be quick before the binmen take it all away. I wouldn't like you to have to go to landfill and search all of that crap for it," Burke said with a sly grin.

"No, quite. I'll go straight away, boss."

"Right, and let me know."

Lawler wasn't inclined to perform this unenviable task single-handedly, so when he got back to the main office where the detectives were just finishing their unexpected morning snack, he said to Amy Sutton, "C'mon, Amy, we have a little job to do for the boss. Oh, and bring some gloves and a few evidence bags."

Sutton had a slightly uneasy feeling about the instruction, but said nothing. She gathered the items Lawler had suggested and caught up with him as he went downstairs to the car park.

"Where are we going?" she said as they exited the building.

"You'll see."

It took them less than fifteen minutes to get back to Moyne Road in Ranelagh. As they turned into the narrow street, they spotted a refuse disposal lorry coming towards them, but it looked as if it hadn't serviced the property they were interested in just yet. Lawler parked in the turning circle.

"The boss wants us to empty out Ortez's recycling bin and see if we can find any packaging material she may have received," Lawler said.

"Nice. At least it's not the compost bin," Sutton said, laughing.

They located the correct green bin stored among the others at the front of number 128. It had big 'Flat 3' writing in white paint on the side of it, distinguishing it from the others packed all along in a row outside the house. Lawler lifted the lid and was pleased to see that it was two-thirds full.

"At least we got here before they did," he said to his colleague, nodding to the approaching bin lorry, "let's empty it out here and see what's what."

He tipped the bin over and lifted up its base so that the contents tumbled out onto the tarmac.

"Thank heavens it's not windy today," Sutton said. She donned blue vinyl gloves and started to rummage through the contents.

As the detectives explored the discarded food packaging and various empty plastic bottles, a woman came out of a nearby house and started remonstrating with them.

"Here! What are you doing? You can't just empty out a bin like that in the roadway. Who are you, anyway?" she shrieked.

Lawler was quite glad of the interruption. He left Sutton examining the rubbish and went to speak to the irate neighbour.

He held up his warrant card and said, "We are from the police, madam. May I ask who you are?"

"My name is Cynthia Green, and I hope you're going to tidy up that mess after you. This is a respectable neighbourhood, you know."

"Yes, of course, Mrs Green. May I ask if you knew any of the occupants of number 128 here?" Lawler gestured towards the house in question.

"Noisy lot. Foreign, I think. I remember when this road was occupied by decent people. That used to be Mr O'Herlihy's place. He was a nice man, even if he was from Cork," Green said. She made a face as if there was a bad smell under her nose as she described her neighbour's place of origin.

"How long has it been in flats?" Lawler said.

"Flats! Is that what you call it? Hovels, more likely. They are packed in like sardines. It's not right, you know. I should have reported it to the council long ago, but I don't suppose they'd do anything about it anyway. What are you looking for anyway?"

"Oh, it's just routine. One of the women that lived in number 128 has been killed and we're investigating."

"Oh my God! Did she die in the house? Well, I never," Green said. She was beginning to enjoy the situation from what Lawler could tell.

"Do you know any of the occupants?"

"No, of course not. I'm a respectable woman, officer, and by the way it's Miss, not Mrs. Of course, I see them coming and going at all hours of the day and night, but we don't socialise if that's what you're asking."

"No, of course not. Well, we must get on. We'll be sure to tidy up when we're done. Good day to you, Miss Green."

The woman didn't reply but went back indoors. Lawler could see the net curtain in her front room twitching as she continued to observe proceedings.

"Anything, Amy?"

"Yes. There's a grey plastic mailing thing here that is addressed to Ortez. It's been torn open, and there's a piece of paper still inside. There's a tracking number on it too, 34694702191375. Isn't that the number we found in her pocket?" Sutton held up a plastic evidence bag containing the specimen for Lawler to see.

"I don't recall the actual number, but we can check it when we get back to the station. Anything else of interest?"

"There's still a slice of pizza here in an old Domino's box if you're feeling peckish," Sutton said with an impish smile.

"Ha ha, very funny. Anything else?"

"No, not that I can see. But have a look yourself just in case I've missed anything."

Lawler and Sutton had one last rummage through the contents of the bin before rounding it up and putting it back in front of the house awaiting collection. They got back into their car and drove back to town.

Chapter Twenty

It was late afternoon when forensics called Moore who had been deskbound all day trying to make sense of the evidence, such as it was, for the deaths of the two Spaniards.

"Hi, Fiona. It's Ruth. I have some results of the DNA tests we were doing on the second Spanish woman and the car."

"Wow! That was quick. What's the story?"

"Yes, we asked for an urgent result. I'll send you over the full report in a few minutes, but I thought you'd like a heads-up on what we found," Ruth said.

Moore was wondering if Ruth would ever get to actually telling her what had been discovered, but she tried not to let her impatience come across.

"And?" Moore said.

"Oh, yes, sorry. The skin particles we took from under Alicia's fingernails don't match the DNA we got from the driver's door handle of the Hyundai. And the tissue on the floor wasn't Alicia's either."

"Have we a match in the system for the DNA of the driver?"

"No, no such luck, I'm afraid."

"Damn! What about the car itself? Has that given up any more evidence? Do we know who owns it, or did own it? I presume it's nicked."

"I'm not sure. I think Keith is working on it with the team. It turns out there was nothing wrong with the car. It was just out of fuel. They'll be finished with it later on. Do you want me to ask Keith to call you?" Ruth said.

"No, it's OK thanks. I'll give him a shout. Can you email me the DNA stuff at once?"

"Yes, sure. Anything else, Fiona?"

"No. Thanks for that. Chat later."

When the call was ended Moore went to bring Aidan Burke up to date on their new evidence.

"Hmm. OK. Do you think this person, whoever he or she may be, is responsible for both murders?" Burke said.

"Looks like it, boss. But we're no further on with an ID for them, or a motive for that matter."

"I have an idea. Maybe our killer isn't Irish. He could be Spanish too, or maybe from somewhere else altogether. Can you run the DNA through the Europol system and see if we get a match? Oh, and what about the UK?"

"Well, they're kinda closed off to us since Brexit. I mean I can try, but I'm not hopeful."

"Tell you what, why don't you contact our friends in the PSNI? They have access to the UK systems, and they are more inclined to be helpful. I can dig out a name for you if you give me a few minutes," Burke said.

"That's a good idea. Let me know when you have someone for me to call."

"Right."

A few minutes later, Burke came out of his office and walked over to where Fiona Moore was seated at her desk.

"There you go. DCI Roddy McClintock. He works out of the Special Operations Branch in Omagh. He's a really sound bloke. Give him a shout." Burke handed Moore a slip of paper with a Northern Ireland phone number on it.

"Thanks, boss, can I mention your name?"

"Yes, of course."

When Burke had gone back to his office, Moore made the call.

After she had introduced herself, she told McClintock what she was hoping he might be able to do for them.

"It's a bit irregular, Sergeant, but I'll see what I can do. Send the DNA profile for my attention to our secure email. And how is that boss of yours keeping? Last time we met we both got on the wrong side of a bottle of Bushmills!"

"Eh... much the same as always, sir. I'll tell him you were asking for him."

"Thanks. I'll get back to you."

Moore forwarded the file containing the DNA profile to the email address that McClintock had provided and hoped he would be able to throw some light on the identity of their suspect. They needed some kind of breakthrough, and soon.

* * *

Lawler and Sutton had driven straight to the forensic lab with their find from the waste bin outside Gabriella Ortez's flat. They went in search of Keith Malone, and found him dressed in a lab coat staring into a microscope with an array of tiny artefacts spread out at his workstation.

"Hi, Keith. Any chance you could have a look at this for us?" Lawler said. He held out the bag containing the mailer.

"Sure. Give it here. What is it and where did you find it?"

Lawler filled Keith in on the item as the technician opened the bag carefully and removed the contents using a forceps.

"Let me take a photograph of the labels and I can get someone working on tracing the origin of the thing. I'll see if I can get any fingerprints or anything off it."

"How long will it take?" Sutton asked.

"About an hour, maybe a little longer. I can give you a call with the results later if you like?"

"Yes, please, Keith. We'd better be getting back," Sutton said. She nudged Dónal Lawler and nodded towards the door.

* * *

Edith Walker was sitting at her desk pouring over a number of spreadsheets. She wasn't happy. No matter how she sliced and diced the data they contained, she just couldn't get a satisfactory result.

Walker had started The World of English some ten years ago. It was one of the first large, dedicated English schools in Dublin, and had been very successful initially. They had rented the premises on Nottingham Street cheaply, as it wasn't a very upmarket area, but it was convenient for transport being not too far from Connolly Station and a good supply of frequent buses passed the end of the road. At first, the market for classes in English for foreigners had not been very price-sensitive, and costs had been modest too. But as the years went by, particularly the latter years, establishment costs had spiralled, and prices had remained much the same due to competition in the market. Energy costs, municipal rates, and particularly insurance premiums had risen alarmingly, and it was getting harder to get teachers for next to nothing, as their rents too had increased dramatically of late.

As Edith Walker stared at the rows and columns in front of her, it became obvious that the school was now running at a considerable loss, despite the numbers of students they were handling, and those losses were beginning to mount.

This was not all news to Walker. She had known for some time that things weren't right. She had borrowed from her bank to the maximum extent that they would tolerate to offset the losses, and she had even put quite an amount of her own money into the business to shore it up. Even the little sideline that she had established some eighteen months previously wasn't making enough of an impact to save her business, but like many entrepreneurs, she was given to unrealistic optimism.

She lifted the phone and dialled the extension for the security guard – a local man that lived on the road and enjoyed a little extra money from working in the evenings. He sat at the front door to repel the local youths who would otherwise have entered the premises and stolen any handy objects such as handbags, purses or wallets left unguarded by the students.

"Hello, Mick. It's Mrs Walker. Could you ask Peter Ledwidge to drop up to see me when he's leaving, please?"

"I'm sorry, ma'am, but Peter has already left."

"Really? I thought he was teaching till eight o'clock?"

Mick was a little embarrassed. He didn't want to get Ledwidge, whom he got on well with, into trouble.

"Eh... he's only gone a few minutes, Mrs Walker. I'm sure you could get him on his mobile phone if it's important."

"Mmm... OK, thanks, Mick. I'll try that."

Walker consulted her own phone for Ledwidge's number and dialled, but after several rings, it went through to voicemail. She elected not to leave a message. He would see the missed call which would be sufficient to alert him to the fact that she was looking for him.

Chapter Twenty-One

The team were in early on Monday morning. Burke called a meeting as soon as they were all there to explore exactly where they were with the two murders and devise some plans.

"OK, everyone, listen up. I'm not happy with the progress we're making on these two cases, and I'm getting heat from upstairs too. The parents of the second girl apparently have connections and they are kicking up a fuss," Burke said.

"You can hardly blame them, boss," Moore said.

"Whatever. But it doesn't make our job any easier. Did you increase the patrols up along the canals last night as I asked you to?"

"Yes, of course, but there's no reports of anything suspicious," Moore said.

"Did you get anything from McClintock in the North?" Burke said.

"No, not yet, boss, I'll give him a nudge later," Moore said.

"What about forensics on the mailer from the bedsit?"

"It came from the Netherlands, sir, we know that. I have someone working on trying to follow it back to an address. There was no trace evidence of what it may have contained, but they did get some fingerprints off the outside of the plastic, though that could have been from the courier company," Lawler said.

"Terrific! But that doesn't sound right to me. Get back on to forensics. Have them go over the inside of it again. There must be some evidence of whatever was in the damn thing. Now, Amy, do you fancy a night out?" Burke said.

Amy Sutton looked around at the rest of the team. She didn't quite know how to react, so she just said, "Sir?"

"Don't worry, Amy, I'm not asking you out on a date! I want you to go to that club, Ozone, tonight. Bring a fella with you if you can find one. Have a good nosy around. See what's going on there – you know, drugs, or whatever. Are you OK with that?"

"Yes, sure. And I won't have any trouble finding someone to accompany me, sir," she said. She looked directly at her boss without the hint of a smile.

"Excellent. Now, Fiona, what are you going to do?"

"I was thinking of having another word with Alicia's two buddies at the school. I think they probably know more than they have told us so far. I think they were close to her, and probably Gabriella too. I want to find out what connects them, apart from the obvious. And I might do a bit of checking on the school too. It all seems to revolve around that place. It's too much of a coincidence for my liking. Fancy tagging along, sir?" Moore said.

"No, not today. You'll do better with the young Spanish women on your own. Get them off the premises, away from the prying eyes of that Walker woman. See if you can open them up. We'll reconvene later on and for an update."

* * *

"Is that DCI McClintock?" Moore said.

"Yes. Ah hello, Sergeant Moore, I was just going to call you. It's about that DNA sample you sent across."

"Yes. Any news, sir?"

"I have as it happens, and it's Roddy by the way. What's your first name?"

"Fiona."

"Well, Fiona, that was very interesting. The sample is from a bloke from Manchester, Darren Roberts, though he also calls himself Darrell Hughes by times. He has quite a rap sheet. He's been in and out of Strangeways a few times. He's not a nice type, not nice at all."

"I see. What was he in for?" Moore said.

"Mostly violence against women. He beat a young woman half to death here five years ago. He nearly got away with it as well. She was too terrified to testify against him, but luckily, we got some good forensics and CCTV evidence that allowed us to put him away. He got six years, but he only served four. He's done a bit of twocking in his time too, but that was when he was younger."

"Twocking?"

"Sorry, car theft. Taking without consent."

"Oh, right, sorry, yes, of course. Any chance you could send me the details? And a mug shot would be a great help too. We're pretty sure he's on our patch and we'd like to talk to him in connection with two killings."

"Yes, of course, no problem. I'm not surprised he's escalated to murder. I'm afraid that's often the way with these types. I hope you catch him soon. Let me know, won't you?" McClintock said.

"Yes, of course, and thanks for your help. We wouldn't have been able to access that information directly since Brexit," Moore said.

"Ah, we all have to live together on this little island of ours, Fiona, no matter what the bloody politicians get up to. I'm glad we were able to help."

"So am I, Roddy. Thanks again. Bye."

Moore went and found Burke in his office and told him what the Northern Ireland policeman had told her.

"Do you want me to circulate the photo with a stop and detain instruction, boss?"

"No, let's not. Not yet anyway. If he knows we're onto him, he'll do a runner. Better to see if we can nab him while he still thinks he's got away with it," Burke said.

"Isn't that a bit risky, sir?"

"Maybe. But if it comes unstuck, it's my call, OK? Write it in your pocket book if you're that concerned."

"It's OK, sir, I trust you. But I'm going to circulate it to the team, if that's all right?"

"Yes, of course."

* * *

Moore asked Amy Sutton to accompany her on the short journey out to Nottingham Street to see the two Spanish girls. When they were in Moore's car, Sutton said, "I've made the arrangements for tonight's visit to Ozone, boss."

"Oh, good. Who are you going with?"

"I have a steady boyfriend, boss. His name is Ian, and before you ask, he's never been in trouble of any kind," Sutton said.

"Oh, nice. How long have you been seeing him, Amy?"

"We've been going out for just over six months. He works on contract in IT support. Just now, he's assigned to a company in the IFSC. Something to do with investments, I think."

"Sounds interesting. Does he have his own place?"

"Yes, he rents a flat in Dundrum, near the shopping centre. I sometimes stay over there, but I keep my own place too. We're not that serious yet."

"No need for me to go out and buy a new hat for now then?" Moore said, smiling.

"No, boss. I'll keep you posted on that one!"

They arrived at The World of English and parked illegally on double yellow lines just outside. The place was busy as ever, with groups of students of various nationalities milling around outside, many of them smoking.

When they got inside, they asked for the two Spanish women by name.

Karla was on the desk as usual, and recognised the detectives.

"If you'd like to take a seat, I'll see if I can locate them for you," Karla said, knowing the drill only too well by now.

Moore and Sutton sat down on the chairs in front of the window and watched as groups of students chattering in strange tongues came and went. After a few minutes, Moore recognised Izzy Hernandez coming down along the long corridor looking very distressed.

"Hello, Izzy. Are you OK?" Moore said when the girl arrived.

"No, please, no, I'm not. It's Maria. She hasn't turned up today, and I can't contact her on her phone. Please, you must help. Maybe she is in danger," the young woman said tearfully.

"Here, sit down, Izzy," Moore said. She found an unused tissue in her pocket and gave it to the girl who dabbed her nose gently with it.

"Now, tell me all about it. When did you last see Maria?" Moore said.

"Yesterday. When college was finished. I wanted to get home to see a programme on the TV about Spain, but she wanted to go and get some pizza, so we parted from each other."

"Do you live together, Isabella?" Sutton asked.

"No. She has a small place quite near here. It's not much, but it's handy for the college, and I'm staying with a family in Stillorgan."

"Have you been around to her place?" Sutton said.

"No. I haven't had time. I've been in classes all day, but it's not like her to have her phone off."

"Did you tell the school about this?" Moore said.

"Yes, I did. I told Karla at lunchtime, but she said that it's not unusual for students to miss a morning of classes and that I should calm down. But what with everything that has happened, I'm really worried. Can you help me?"

"Yes, of course. Why don't we go around to Maria's place and see if she is there? She could just be asleep," Moore said.

Hernandez seemed to be a little reassured by Moore's suggestion and she picked up her bag and stood up.

"We can walk, if you like. It's not very far," Hernandez said.

"No. Let's take the car. I don't want it to be towed away. It's badly parked."

Moore followed Izzy Hernandez's directions out onto the North Strand Road where she turned right back towards the city.

"Here it is, just here," Hernandez said as they bumped over the ramps in the road on Clonmore Terrace. She pointed to a small, red-bricked cottage that opened up onto the footpath with a dark green door and a single window to its right-hand side.

Moore pulled the car up and they all got out. Moore went to the door and knocked firmly, then stood back.

"Is this all one dwelling, Isabella?"

"No. There are two little apartments here. Maria has her own small kitchen and a tiny shower room as well as a bedroom where you can sit and watch the TV. Her apartment is at the back."

Moore looked at Sutton and nodded. The junior detective got the message and went off to find the laneway that would lead her to the rear of the terrace of modest houses. Moore knocked again on the front door, but there was no response.

"It looks like she's not in, Isabella. Try her phone again, will you?"

Izzy dialled Maria's number on her iPhone.

After a few moments she said, "No, it's just voicemail again. I must have left loads of messages now. Where is she?" she said, beginning to sound a little desperate.

They were still standing on the footpath outside the house when Sutton returned.

"Nothing, boss. There's a gate and a small yard at the back. The gate was open and I went in, but I couldn't see anything. It's too dark inside."

"OK, well, never mind," Moore said. "Izzy, do you want to go back to the college?"

"No. I'm going to go home. I can't concentrate. Can you leave me at the Luas?"

"Yes, sure. Give me your phone number and here's my card. Let me know if you hear from her, and I'll do the same. OK?"

"Yes, OK."

Chapter Twenty-Two

Inspector Aidan Burke was sitting at his desk pondering his fate. If he did have to transfer to the sticks for a few years to let things in the city quieten down, where would he go? He didn't like the sound of Cork, although that's where Heffernan would likely want to send him. No, Wexford or Waterford would be more to his liking, but then again, maybe he wouldn't get a choice.

He was deep in his imagination trying to process the thought of the whole thing when his phone jangled on his desk.

"Burke," he said.

"Inspector, it's Keith here from The Park. I thought you'd like to know we found a piece of paper underneath the mat in the boot of the car we brought in from the canal. It's a receipt for car parts. They aren't for that car; they are clutch parts for a VW Golf."

"Hi, Keith. And I need to know this, why?"

"Well, the receipt is made out to a JK Motors, and there's an address. In fact, it looks more like an invoice than a receipt."

"Nice one, Keith. Give me the details please."

Burke noted down the address for JK Motors which he recognised as being somewhere up behind Smithfield Square on the north side of the river.

"Oh, and there's more, sir. The registration number that was on the car is from a Mercedes Sprinter van that was scrapped more than two years ago, according to the licensing folks."

"Excellent. Thanks, Keith. I'll take it from here."

Burke tore the page containing the details out of his jotter and went in search of Dónal Lawler who was just addressing a freshly brewed mug of tea in the little kitchenette at the back of the open plan.

"Ah, Dónal, the very man. We need to go out for a drive. Are you ready?" Burke said.

"I was just about to have this tea, boss. Can we hold on a few minutes?" Lawler said.

"Never mind your tea. I'll buy you a pint if this pans out. C'mon!"

* * *

JK Motors occupied a scruffy but capacious yard on Nicholas Street, close to what had been Smithfield Market. The market had been demolished a few years back, and the place was now a gentrified square of modern apartments, chic eateries and various other shops and businesses. But somehow, although it was close to the recent new development, Nicholas Street had escaped the builders. It was comprised of a few semi-derelict warehouses and the yard that housed the scrap car business.

Burke drove his eight-year-old Mercedes into the greasy premises and stopped between two towers of rusting hulks. An all-black German shepherd announced their arrival with fierce barking and baring of teeth, but Burke observed, thankfully, that the animal was retained close to a filthy portacabin by a stout chain. As they got out of the car, an overweight man in his late fifties, dressed in a dark blue boiler suit that was in dire need of a wash, emerged from the cabin and stood consoling his pet.

Burke and Lawler got out of the car and walked over.

"I'll give ye two grand for it. Not a penny more. Those things can be awful trouble when they get to that age," the man said.

"And who might you be?" Burke said, not at all amused by the man's offer.

"More to the point, who the hell are you?" he replied.

Burke held up his warrant card.

"DI Burke, and this is Detective Garda Lawler. Do I have to ask again?"

"Jude Kelly, sir. Sole proprietor of this great emporium," the man said sweeping his arm around in an arc, "and what can I do for you two men today?"

"We are making enquiries about a silver Hyundai saloon that we believe may have come from here. Have you sold one of those to anyone recently?" Burke said.

"I don't sell entire cars here, Inspector. We break them up, and sell the parts. Then we crush what's left and sell it on for recycling. I'm very environmentally friendly, you know," the man said with a grin.

"So how come we found an invoice for parts for a Golf in the boot of said Hyundai then with your name on it?" Lawler said.

Before the man could reply, Burke went on, "And how come the car was registered as a Mercedes Sprinter van cleverly disguised as a Hyundai Accent?"

"You'd better come in," Kelly said. All traces of mirth had left his now sullen face. He turned towards the portacabin.

Burke looked at the dog who hadn't taken its eyes off the two detectives since they arrived. He reckoned that the animal was within striking distance if they decided to go into the hut.

"No, we'll stay here, Mr Kelly. Look, have you seen this guy at all recently?" Burke took a photocopy of the image of Darren Roberts that McClintock had sent them from Northern Ireland and showed it to Kelly.

"Can't say that I have," Kelly said.

"Then, let me jog your memory for you, Mr Kelly. He would have been in here less than a week ago looking for anything that still drives and offering cash, no questions asked. He may even have bought a Toyota Avensis from you before that too. Ring any bells?"

Kelly thought for a moment.

"Would he have had kind of an English accent, maybe?"

"Maybe. What do you remember about him?"

"He was quite young; I'd say in his twenties. Not very tall. He said he had two hundred euro if I had anything that was still driving. The old Hyundai drove in, so I reckoned it could drive out again, so I sold it to him. That's it," Kelly said.

"And what about the plates?" Lawler said.

"I dunno. We take all the plates off when the cars come in and put them over there in that big bin. I just grabbed the first two that fitted and put them back on the car. He didn't seem too bothered."

Burke looked at Lawler and shook his head in amazement.

"And had he been in here before?" Lawler went on.

"I think you're right. He might have bought an old Avensis from me before. I can't remember, to be honest," Kelly said.

Burke was at a bit of a loss as to what to do with Jude Kelly. If he closed him down, which he was quite entitled to do, they might lose a valuable contact. But the man was breaking all sorts of laws. Burke thought for a few moments in silence and then said, "Look, Jude, I can only guess at the number of laws you have broken here, but I'm not too bothered about that for now. We need to find this guy, and you may be able to help. If he comes in again, I want to know immediately, and I mean at once. And I want you to keep a record of exactly what you've sold him, and the registration number you've put on the car. Is that clear?"

"I suppose. What's he done anyway?" Kelly said.

"You don't want to know, trust me."

Burke handed the scrap merchant a business card and turned to walk back to the sanctity of his own car, with Lawler following behind, somewhat bemused.

"Do you think that was wise, boss?" Lawler said when they were on their way back to the station.

"What choice do we have? That bloke is the only link we have to our suspect. But don't worry, I'm not finished with Jude Kelly yet. We can always go back for a visit when all this is over," Burke said, grinning.

Lawler said nothing. He was trying to figure out how he could make Burke's promise of a pint come good.

Chapter Twenty-Three

Amy Sutton had changed her appearance almost beyond recognition. She was dressed in party clothes – a very short skirt, and a black cotton top that was cut in a deep U-shape revealing the lacy trim at the top of her black bra.

"How do I look?" she said to Ian, her boyfriend, as she came down the stairs and landed in the hall.

"Fabulous, love, amazing."

It was just the reaction she was hoping for. In truth, Detective Garda Amy Sutton had truly transformed her appearance. Her dark brown hair shone as it bounced playfully on her shoulders; her face was beautifully made up, and her eyes sparkled brightly. This woman was dressed to impress!

As they sat into the back of the taxi that would take them to Ozone, Sutton said to her partner, "When we get here, we need to split up. Keep an eye on me from a distance, but I have things to do. Is that OK?"

"I guess. What have you to do?"

"Just some stuff for the job. I'll be fine, but if you see anyone bothering me, step in."

"OK. Do you want me to punch the guy's lights out?" Ian said.

"Eh... no. That won't be necessary. Anyway, I'd have to arrest you and put you in handcuffs and take you down to the station."

"Ooooh, kinky!"

"Behave, you pervert," she said. She snuggled into him and gave him a nice warm kiss.

* * *

They arrived at Ozone at around ten-thirty. The place was just starting to get going, and when they went inside, they could see that there were quite a few foreigners milling about. They made for the bar and Ian ordered for them both. Amy was just drinking soda water, but Ian had a pint, getting a bit of a surprise when the bill came to over €10.

When they had their drinks, Ian drifted away discreetly and took up a vantage point against the side wall of the premises where he could still see Amy, but wasn't overtly observing her. Amy had managed to conceal a very small Panasonic Lumix camera in her purse. She had programmed it so that the flash was disabled, and had loaded it with a beefy SD card that would allow her to record almost an hour of video footage before it filled up. If she could just manage to keep it out of sight she could get some useful evidence, though needless to say, she hadn't told any of her superior officers about the subterfuge.

At what must have been close to eleven-thirty, a group of young women came into the club. They were chattering to each other in Spanish, and they were all dressed in skimpy clothes, showing a lot of flesh. They went to the bar. It was obvious to Sutton that they were known to the barman who dispensed a variety of drinks to the group, but didn't appear to charge them anything.

As they stood at the bar drinking, a Middle-Eastern-looking man approached and slid his arm around the bare waist of one of the girls. She turned to him and smiled broadly before looking to the ever-attentive barman who nodded almost imperceptibly. Then the couple moved away, and from what Amy could see in the gloom of the nightclub, they disappeared through a door that was painted black near the back of the premises.

This process was repeated several times until the entire group of giggling girls had disappeared. Then, Amy herself was approached by another Middle Eastern type – this one considerably older. He put his hand on her bottom and tried to draw her close, but she was well able to repel his advances, and after a few more attempts at over-familiarity, he skulked off to try his luck elsewhere.

Sutton had recorded much of what was going on. She held the camera down low, and panned around the club unobtrusively. She had captured the moment when the Spanish girls started to re-emerge from the concealed door, accompanied by their male partners who then melted into the crowd and disappeared. After about half an hour, the Spaniards were all back at the bar enjoying fresh drinks, apparently free, and chatting away. They occasionally burst into fits of giggles, but it wasn't long before the process she had observed earlier was repeated.

By twelve-thirty the club was becoming very crowded, and Sutton was having difficulty keeping track of her quarry. Deciding that she had enough to inform the team back at the station the following day, she made her way over to where Ian was patiently standing by.

"Sorry about that, love. Are you bored silly?" Sutton said.

"No, I'm fine. I enjoyed watching all the goings-on, and those Spanish girls are very hot," he said with a big silly grin.

"Don't you dare! Looks to me like they are all hookers. I had no idea that this place was a knocking shop. Can we get out of here now?"

"Yeah, sure. I've been nursing this pint since we came in. It's gone flat and warm. Yuk."

Sutton took Ian's hand. He deposited the largely consumed pint on a shelf and they left the place, walking back out onto the quays where there were lots of taxis to take them home. Once they were seated comfortably in the back of a very clean cab, Ian said, "Well, did you manage to get any decent stuff on your little camera?"

Sutton took the device out of her purse, turned it on, and pressed 'play'. Although there were some scenes that were blurred as people had walked across in front of her while she was recording, she did manage to capture some excellent footage of the Spanish girls and some of their 'clients' as they came and went through the secret door. She also had a good few images of the barman whom she assumed was fully complicit in the business.

"Some of those chicks look to be under 18 to me," Ian said.

"Less talk of chicks, please, Ian. These are young women, but I agree, some of them do look to be underage. That makes it interesting."

"How do you mean?"

"Well, if they are under 18, then technically they are children, and that brings a whole new dimension to the thing," Sutton said.

"Wow! I see what you mean."

When they got back to Sutton's apartment, she said, "I think I'll just see if I can print off some still pictures from the camera. It will save time tomorrow. Do you mind?"

"No, that's fine. I'm pretty tired anyway. I think I'll get off. I have an early start in the morning."

They said good night, and agreed to call each other the following day.

Amy removed the SD card from the little Panasonic camera and pushed it into the slot on the side of her laptop computer. She loaded a video editing program on the PC and started moving through the recording that she had made earlier. It wasn't long before she came to some clear images of the girls at the bar. She paused the recording and used the software to capture some still images of the Spaniards, sending them to her inkjet printer, which whirred and clicked before emitting some rather good A4-sized pictures.

Amy continued the work on the video, and after an hour had managed to collect nearly twenty photos, some of which showed the men involved in the matter clearly. She also had two very good pictures of the barman that could be used to identify him beyond doubt.

Pleased with her efforts, she turned off the printer, shut down the laptop, and placed her evidence in a large manila envelope, ready to take to work the following day.

Chapter Twenty-Four

The mood in Store Street Garda station was glum the following morning when the detectives assembled. Moore took charge of the briefing.

"OK, well firstly, is there any news on the missing girl, anyone?"

No one said anything, so Moore went on, "That will be a 'no' then. Right, we need to escalate this to a full missing persons enquiry now. Do we have a decent photo of the woman?"

"I don't think so, Sarge, but I can get onto the school and see what they have, or her friends may have some selfies they could send us," Sutton said.

"Yes, good idea, Amy. Get onto them as soon as we've finished here. Dónal, what did you and the inspector get from the car place, if anything?" Moore said.

Lawler filled the group in on their visit to JK Motors.

"I see," Moore said. "Well, that means that this Darren Roberts must be our prime suspect for the murders then. But what I need to know is what motive had he for these killings. There seems to be no rationale that I can think of. Anyone got any ideas?"

"I may have something, boss," Sutton said.

"Yes, Amy, what is it?"

"Last night I went with my boyfriend to Ozone. After we'd been there for an hour or so, a group of young Spanish women came in. And, not to put too fine a point on it, it looks as if they were selling themselves to punters – mostly Middle Eastern men."

"Christ! Are you serious, Amy?"

"Well, that's what it looked like to us. And the barman seems to be involved in it too. I managed to get some pictures," Sutton said. She held up the envelope containing the photographs she had produced the previous night at home.

Moore took the envelope from Sutton and opened it, removing the A4 sheets from within. She paged through them for a moment.

"These are pretty clear. I wonder if Isabella Hernandez would recognise them?" Moore said.

"It's definitely worth a try, boss. Should I go around to the school and see if I can get an ID for them?"

"Yes. I think I'll come with you, but before we go, Dónal, can you start a trawl for this Roberts guy. You know, all the usual. See if any of your snouts have heard anything, and let's make it public as well. See if we can flush him out. Don't forget to cover the airports and ferries too. He may try to dash back to the UK once he knows we're onto him. Oh, and is there any news of the CCTV we asked for in the lane outside Ozone?" Moore said.

"Yes, Sarge. Dublin City Council say there's a camera further down the lane. They've given us a live feed from it. I have one of the civilian support staff keeping an eye on it, and of course we're recording it too," Lawler said.

"Great. Let me know if anything strange pops up on it, won't you?"

"Yes, of course."

"Right. Well, let's make Maria Gomez our number one priority for today, followed by Roberts or Hughes or whatever he's calling himself."

"Yes, Sarge," they said in unison.

The phone began to ring, and Amy Sutton got up to answer it. When she had finished the brief call, she spoke to Moore, "Sorry, Sarge, but Isabella Hernandez is in reception and is asking for you."

"OK, thanks, Amy. I'd better go and see what she wants. There could be some news of Maria."

Burke grunted. He wasn't too happy to have the meeting interrupted, but he had to admit that the girl could have some meaningful information. Moore got up and left the room.

Hernandez looked much less upset than she had been the last time Moore had seen her. Moore greeted her, and took her through to one of the interview rooms.

"So, Izzy, what can I do for you?" Moore said.

"It's Maria, Sergeant. I had a text message from her very early this morning. It seems she is back in Spain."

"I see. Do you have your phone with you?"

"Yes, of course," the young woman said. She reached into her jacket pocket and removed a newish-looking iPhone. She fiddled with the thing for a moment before handing it to Moore with the screen facing the detective.

Moore took the device and tried to read the message, but it was, naturally, in Spanish. However, immediately following the message there was a selfie of Maria showing that she had two black eyes and a split lip, as well as a bruise on her cheek.

"What does the message say, Isabella?" Moore said.

"It says she was beaten up at the nightclub. She is very frightened. That's why she ran to the airport and got on the first flight to Spain that she could get."

"I see. And does she say who beat her up?"

"No. But now I am scared too," Hernandez said.

"Listen, Isabella, what exactly is going on here? What is the connection between the English school and the nightclub?"

"I can't say anything. They will come after me too and maybe do worse to me."

"Who will come after you? You know we can protect you if you think you are in danger."

"No, it's no use. They will find a way. Look what happened to Maria and the other girls. I will be killed!"

"Not if we provide you with protection, Isabella. You will be quite safe. Look, can you stay here for a minute or two. I want to go upstairs and get someone to come and examine your phone to see if we can trace where exactly Maria was when she sent the message. And I need to get that photograph downloaded too. It's evidence."

"Yes, OK."

Moore left the room to see if she could find anyone who spoke Spanish anywhere in the building. She also wanted someone with good technical knowledge to properly explore Hernandez's phone. She wasn't completely convinced by the story she had been told.

She was in luck. There was a small technical unit in Store Street Garda station, and when she went there and asked, a young officer by the name of Craig Walsh said that he had a smattering of Spanish, and he could examine the phone too. Moore led the way back downstairs to where she had left the Spaniard, but when she got to the room, it was empty.

Moore went to the front desk and spoke to the duty sergeant.

"Where did the young woman I was speaking to go?" she said.

"Oh, hello, Sergeant. She left a few minutes ago. She said you were finished with her."

"Damn! Did you see which way she went?"

"No, sorry."

Moore dashed out onto the street to see if she could see where Isabella had gone, but there was no sign of the woman anywhere.

* * *

"Well?" Burke said as Fiona Moore re-joined the briefing.

"She's gone," Moore said. She went on to explain how the young Spaniard had left the building.

"Terrific!" Burke said.

"Well, at least we know Maria Gomez is not another murder victim, boss."

"Do we now? That could easily have been faked, or perhaps she sent the message with a knife against her throat. Get onto the airport. Find out if she really did leave for Spain either last night or this morning. And while you are at it, get the airlines to alert us if Hernandez tries to book a flight to Spain. Meantime, get someone around to her place and see if we can get her back!" Burke said.

Seeing that her boss was not impressed with her, Moore left quietly to do his bidding.

"Now, what else have we got?" Burke said to the remaining members of the team.

"I was watching the CCTV footage from the camera the council have further down the lane, boss. I was looking back on some of the footage, and last Friday at just after eleven, guess who could be seen entering the club?" Lawler said.

"Go on," Burke said.

"None other than Mrs Walker, the owner of The World of English."

"Bloody hell!" Burke said. "I think we need to go and have a little chat with that lady, don't you?"

"Looks like it, boss," Lawler said.

Chapter Twenty-Five

On the way around to The World of English in the car, Burke said to Lawler, "What the blazes do you think is going on, Dónal? I can't make head nor tail of it."

"I think there may be more than one thing going on. It looks as if some of the young women are working as hookers at the nightclub. Whether or not Mrs Walker is involved remains to be seen, but she certainly has some connection to Ozone. Then there's the business about the mysterious package that arrived from the Netherlands, not to mention the killing of the two girls along the canal. It's a jigsaw," Lawler said.

"But do you think it's all connected?"

"Hard to tell just yet. I'd like to establish a motive for the murders. That's the missing piece. Why did someone feel the need to bump off two young Spanish students? I mean, even if they were prostituting themselves, it's hardly a reason to kill them, is it?" Lawler said.

"No, I agree. There's more to it than that. But I'll be damned if I know what. Hang on, here we are. Maybe Walker can give us some information."

Burke drove up to the school steps, but as usual there was no parking available.

"God dammit, this place is bloody impossible," Burke said. He moved the car on towards the end of the narrow road hoping that there might be some nook or cranny he could leave the car. At the far side of the school building there was a narrow lane. It was too narrow for Burke to enter, but he used it to turn his vehicle. As he swung the nose into the opening, Lawler noticed that there was a dark red motorcycle parked in the laneway tethered to a pole supporting a traffic sign prohibiting entry. Burke was too busy manoeuvring the car in the tight space to notice it, but Lawler, ever observant, made a mental note of the number plate. Burke finally found somewhere to abandon his car where it wasn't completely blocking the thoroughfare, even though it was at least half up on the footpath. The two Gardaí got out and went into the school.

Inside, Karla was seated at the reception desk as usual. The detectives approached.

"We're here to see Mrs Walker, Karla. Is she in?" Burke said.

Karla looked up at the two men and sensed that Burke in particular was unlikely to be put off his mission.

"I'll just give her a call and see if she is available," Karla said. She picked up the phone and dialled, turning away from the two detectives and whispering into the instrument. A moment later, she turned back to face them and replaced the receiver.

"I'm afraid Mrs Walker is busy just now. She asked if you could come back in the afternoon, maybe after four?"

"That's fine, Karla. We'll just wait down along here until she pops out for a coffee or something. We won't keep her long." Burke and Lawler walked away from the desk.

"But what about…" Karla started to say, but realised that they were ignoring her.

Burke walked down the long corridor in front of him with Lawler following closely behind. When he reached the office with Walker's nameplate, he just opened the door and barged straight in. Walker was seated at her desk and looked up at the unexpected intrusion.

"Good morning, Mrs Walker. We need a word."

"I'm busy. I told you. Come back later," she said frostily.

"I don't think so," Burke said calmly. "We need to talk now, or I could just arrest you and take you down to Store Street. Of course, I'd have to have you led out in handcuffs in front of your staff and students. It might not look too good," Burke said, smirking at his colleague.

"On what charge?" Walker said.

"Don't worry, I'll think of something suitable. What do you say, Dónal, 'obstruction', do you think that would do it?"

"Sounds about right, boss."

Walker looked at DI Burke for a few moments trying to read his expression. Was he serious, or was he just being a prick? After another minute of tense silence elapsed, she uttered the single word, "Sit."

The detectives sat down, and Burke waited for a couple of minutes before starting his questioning. He wanted to let the tension build a little further.

"Mrs Walker, are you aware that several of your students are hiring themselves out to men, presumably for sex?" Burke said.

"What? No, of course not. But whatever they get up to in their own time is none of my business. There's nothing like that going on here, that much I can tell you," the woman said indignantly.

"How do you know?" Lawler chimed in.

"Of course I know. I'm in charge here in case you had forgotten."

"Yes, but how would you know that there's no hanky-panky going on here from time to time? After all, you can't be everywhere at once, now can you?" Lawler said.

Walker put down her pen and looked Dónal Lawler right between the eyes.

"What have you really come here for? If you're going to talk nonsense, then you had better leave. I have work to be getting on with."

"What do you know of a nightclub called Ozone, Mrs Walker?"

"Do I look like the type of woman who frequents nightclubs, Inspector?" she said.

"You haven't answered my question, Mrs Walker. I'll ask again, what do you know of a nightclub called Ozone?" Burke said.

"I've already told you. Nothing. Why would I?"

Burke said nothing, but reached into his inside pocket and took out a sheet of A4 paper that was folded in quarters. He made a point of slowly unfolding the paper, looking at it, and then turning it around and putting it down in front of the woman, facing her.

"This is a still picture taken from a CCTV camera outside Ozone yesterday morning. It shows you entering the club. As you can see, it is date-and-time-stamped. We have a corresponding photograph of you leaving the club about twenty minutes later, also date-and-time-stamped. Care to explain?" Burke said.

Mrs Walker thought for a moment, and then said quietly, "No comment."

Burke nodded at Lawler and stood up.

"Mrs Edith Walker, I'm arresting you on suspicion of being involved in prostitution contrary to the Sexual Offences Act of 2017," Lawler said. He went on to recite the remainder of the well-practiced mantra while Burke summoned a Garda car from Store Street to come and take their suspect away.

On the way out of the building, Walker instructed Karla to get hold of Janet O'Sullivan and get a solicitor to attend Store Street Garda station as soon as possible.

Before leaving the school, Burke gave some instructions to Lawler.

"You stay here. Talk to O'Sullivan. Try and get her to give up the latest financial information about the school voluntarily. Frighten her a bit if you have to – you know the drill. See if you can get hold of bank statements, you know, all that sort of stuff. And see if she'll let you have a go over Walker's office too. If you're invited to have a look around, then we don't need a warrant, but be careful, don't mess it up. There could be evidence that we will rely on later, and I don't want some smart-arsed lawyer going all 'inadmissible' on us."

"OK, boss. I'll be back in an hour or so. I'd like to be in on the interview with her. Can you hold off?"

"Yeah, no problem. There's no rush anyway. Best to let her sweat for a while, don't you think?"

Lawler just smiled.

Chapter Twenty-Six

Fiona Moore had very little luck with the airlines. She was given a number of different excuses, from 'our systems are down at the moment' to 'you need a warrant for that kind of information, Sergeant', and she was becoming very frustrated.

Amy Sutton could see Moore across the room, and sensed her impatience. Indeed, she could hardly miss it, as Moore's language was deteriorating fast, and she had started to emit regular expletives. Sutton got up and went over to Moore's desk.

"What's up, Sarge?"

"God give me strength, Amy. These bloody airlines!" Moore went on to explain her predicament, and that she was very anxious to have some information for Inspector Burke before he returned as she had slipped up earlier letting the Spanish girl get away.

"Hang on. I have an idea."

Moore looked on as Amy Sutton consulted an online directory of government services.

"Here. Let me try this," Sutton said.

She lifted the phone and after a few false starts, got through to a senior officer at Dublin Airport's immigration department. She explained what she was looking for, and Moore could hear her giving out her contact details over the phone. When she had finished the call, she turned to Moore.

"Immigration scan all the passports these days. The scans are kept online for a week or so, and that guy says he can set off a search for Gomez to see if she departed in the last little while. He'll be back to me in an hour."

"Thanks, Amy. Why didn't I think of that?" Moore said.

"No worries, Sarge. I'll let you know when he calls."

"Thanks, Amy. Nice one."

Moore relaxed a bit when Amy Sutton had gone back to her own desk. At least she might have something positive to tell her boss when he returned. But before she could go and get herself a coffee now that the heat was off, so to speak, her phone rang.

"Is that Sergeant Moore?"

"Yes, who's this, please?"

"Hello, Fiona. It's Roddy McClintock here from the PSNI. How's things?"

"Oh, hello, Roddy. Hmm... only so-so."

"Hmm... that good, eh? Listen, I just wanted to have a word with you about Darren Roberts, alias Darrell Hughes. I did a bit more digging. Apparently, there's an arrest warrant out for him from Manchester," McClintock said.

"Oh? What's he done?"

"The local boys in Manchester were out on patrol and spotted him driving a stolen car. They managed to stop him after a short pursuit. Seems he had no driving licence, road tax, or insurance either. But when they were at the roadside, he kicked one of the officers in the groin and made off. The car was found burnt out on waste ground the following morning, and of course no sign of your man. So, the boys in Manchester would really like to have a word."

"Yes, I can see why. No sign of him up North at all?"

"Nope. Nothing. But I just wanted to call you to let you know. If you do manage to find him, hang on to him for us, won't you?"

"Don't worry, Roddy, if we get our hands on him, he won't be going anywhere. Anyway, how does all this arrest warrant stuff work since you guys left the EU?"

"Badly, that's how. It's a mess, to be honest, and the Home Office are making it worse every day. But we are finding ways around the red tape as time goes on. The most important thing is to apprehend the little bugger. Then we can figure out who gets him first, and for what."

"Sounds good to me, Roddy. I'll let you know if he turns up."

"Likewise, Fiona. Thanks. Bye."

"Bye, Roddy."

* * *

Dónal Lawler was getting on well at the school. Janet O'Sullivan was being helpful, once she had got over the shock of her boss being taken away by uniformed Gardaí. O'Sullivan was obviously a woman of principle. Lawler calculated that she probably went to church every Sunday, and did her very best to live a decent life. Lawler had been careful about the amount of information he had disclosed to the woman, but he had made it clear that there was at least a possibility that Mrs Walker was involved in some unsavoury goings-on.

"I have all the financial information you need here, Sergeant," she said to Lawler as they sat in her office over cups of tea and biscuits.

"Thanks, Ms O'Sullivan. But before I get into all that, can you tell me in your own words how well the school has been doing lately?"

"We have very good attendance, Sergeant. The school can accommodate 180 students when it is fully booked. We usually have between 150 and 160 places occupied at any one time, spread over several classes. And then there is the evening courses as well. We operate from 6:00 p.m. to 8:00 or 8:30 p.m. four nights a week. Mrs Walker manages that personally. She collects the fees and pays the tutors herself."

"What happens to the balance of the cash?" Lawler said.

"I don't ask, Sergeant. It's none of my business."

"So, she could be pocketing that herself?"

"As I said, it's none of my business. I'm employed to administer the college by day. Whatever happens after hours is beyond my remit."

"And what about the financials of the day school, Ms O'Sullivan?"

O'Sullivan thought for a moment before answering.

"I was hoping you wouldn't ask that, Sergeant," she said. She took another sip of tea.

"But now that I have…?"

"You have to understand, we are in a very competitive business. And costs just keep going up and up. You wouldn't believe how much our insurance premiums are, and then there's energy costs, cleaning, computer maintenance, and the tutors have had several increases recently. They are mostly living in rented accommodation, and their rents have been going up steeply too."

"So, what's the bottom line?"

"It's red, I'm afraid. Look, if I tell you something in confidence, will you promise not to let Mrs Walker know I told you?"

"Well, I'll try, but I can't make any promises I'm afraid."

Lawler could sense the woman's discomfort. She was torn between loyalty to her employer and the desire to tell the truth to the police, whose authority she had never questioned at any stage of her life. Lawler waited for her to resolve the conflict.

"A few months ago, Mrs Walker, Edith, took me aside and told me that the school was in trouble for money. She said that she had been putting in quite large amounts from her personal savings to shore it up, but that she couldn't go on doing that. She asked me if I had any spare cash that I could lend the business. She said she would give me shares in it."

"What did you do?"

"I told her I wasn't interested in shares, but that I had some savings, and I could lend the school some money as long as there was a plan for it to be returned to me at some stage. She said not to worry, that she had an idea that would generate extra income, and that the money I put in would be short-term only," O'Sullivan said.

"And?"

"I cashed in some Savings Certificates that I had had for years, and a Government Bond, and I raised €15,000. Paperwork was drawn up, and I lodged the money to the school's account. Mrs Walker was very grateful. She said I had saved the place from going under, and I would be repaid as soon as matters started to improve, and that I could expect a healthy bonus as well."

"What was her plan to generate extra income?"

"She never said, and I didn't like to ask. After all, it was none of my business."

"Did anything change after that; I mean in the way the school was run?" Lawler said.

"No, not really. I did notice that we started to get a lot of younger Spanish girls. And the strange thing was that they appeared to have quite good English when they arrived, which I thought was a bit odd. But I didn't think much of it, to be honest."

"Have you received any of your loan back at all?" Lawler said.

O'Sullivan shuffled uncomfortably in her seat.

"No, not yet. But I'm sure I will eventually," she said very unconvincingly.

"What do you know about a nightclub down by the quays called Ozone, Ms O'Sullivan?" Lawler asked.

"Sorry, what did you call it again?"

Lawler wondered if the woman was playing for time so that she could think up something sensible to say in answer to his question.

"Ozone. You know, like the gas in the atmosphere," Lawler said.

"Nothing. I've never heard of the place," O'Sullivan said.

"Are you sure, Ms O'Sullivan? It's important," Burke said.

"Oh, wait a minute. I think there's a poster on the noticeboard in the lobby with something like that on it. Yes, that's right. They do a Spanish night, I think."

"Have you ever been to the place?" Lawler said.

"No, of course not. Do I look like the kind of person that frequents nightclubs, officer?"

"So, Mrs Walker has never asked you to go there for an errand or anything, say, to collect or deliver anything?"

"No, she hasn't. And I'd be surprised if she had any association with such an outfit too. Why do you ask?" Janet O'Sullivan said.

"It's just a line of enquiry we are following. No need for you to worry about it. Just one last thing, Ms O'Sullivan, then we'll leave you in peace. Have you noticed any difference in the Spanish students that have been coming here recently, apart from the fact that they are younger and already have some English?" Lawler said.

"No, I can't say that I have. They are all very bubbly and of course lovely-looking too, but I can't say I've noticed anything special."

"Right. Well, thank you for your time, Janet. We'll keep what you have told us to ourselves if we can."

Lawler left the woman's office, and walked towards the entrance. As he approached the door, Lawler turned to Karla and said, "Karla. Do you know who owns the red motorcycle parked in the lane?" Lawler gestured to the side of the building where he had seen the bike earlier.

"Oh, that. Yes, I do. That's Peter's."

"Peter?" Lawler said.

"Yes, Peter Ledwidge. He teaches here quite often. I've been hoping he would take me for a spin on it sometime, but he doesn't seem too bothered."

"Thanks, Karla. Bye now."

Chapter Twenty-Seven

Jude Kelly was having a small crisis of conscience. On the one hand, he had no desire for any more contact with the Gardaí than was absolutely necessary. But on the other hand, this little scrote was obviously up to no good, and he didn't want to be implicated if the little fecker got himself into real trouble. He consulted his trusty German shepherd about his dilemma, but got a totally neutral response from the animal, who just licked his hand and looked up at him with big soulful eyes.

"Fair enough, then. I'd better make the call," Kelly said to himself reaching for the grease-encrusted telephone that was sitting in amongst a pile of papers on his so called 'desk'. He rummaged in the detritus and found the card Burke had given him. He dialled the number.

"Burke," came the reply when the phone was answered.

"Ah, 'tis yourself, sir. It's Jude Kelly here from JK Motors in Nicholas Street."

"Oh, yes, Mr Kelly. What can I do for you?"

"Well, it's more a case of what I can do for you, Inspector." Then Kelly remained silent.

"And what's that then, Mr Kelly?"

"Well, you know your man you were enquiring about? That young fella that bought the Hyundai off me."

"Yes, I do. What about him?" Burke felt like he was pulling teeth.

"He was only back in here, wasn't he?"

"I see. And when exactly was this, Mr Kelly?"

"Oh, yesterday. I was just about to close up for the day, so it must have been close to five o'clock. I don't keep the yard open once it gets dark, you know, you could get injured walking around here with all the sharp edges on the old cars."

"And you waited till now to call me, why?"

"Ah, I was a bit busy. You know what it's like."

"Anyway, what did the lad want?" Burke said.

"He was after a car again. He's getting through them at a fierce rate altogether. I can't imagine what he's doing with them, can you?" Kelly said.

"And did you sell him a car?"

"I did of course. Isn't that why I'm calling you?"

Burke reached for a notebook and pen.

"Go on then. What type of car? What colour? And what number does it have now?"

"It's an old Polo. Well past its sell-by date, to be honest, but still going. Oh, wait a minute now, I have the number here somewhere."

Burke could hear the man shuffling papers on his desk.

"What colour is the vehicle, Mr Kelly?"

"God, it's a kind of dark blue, but the bonnet is off a white one, and the passenger's door is the same. Ah, here we are. It has ZS 8667 on it now."

Burke rolled his eyes to heaven.

"Any other distinguishing features?" Burke said.

Kelly didn't get the irony.

"No, no. That's about it. It shouldn't be too hard to find looking like that," Kelly said.

"Right. Well, thanks for the call, Mr Kelly. It's a pity you didn't think to let me know earlier though."

“Good luck now,” the man said and the line went dead.

Burke left his office and found Sutton sitting at her desk just finishing a call with the immigration department at Dublin Airport.

“Amy, could you look up this car reg for me? I want to know what vehicle it belongs to. And then put out an all-points notice for a mostly blue VW Polo with that number. Stop and detain,” Burke said.

“Eh... sorry, sir. Mostly blue?”

“Oh, sorry, yes, I should have said. It has a white bonnet and a white nearside door, but the rest of it is blue, or so I was told.”

“Oh, OK. And by the way, that was Dublin Airport on the phone. Maria Gomez left on a flight to London, but they couldn’t say whether she went on to Spain or not.”

“OK, thanks, Amy.”

Sutton turned back to her PC and started tapping out instructions.

* * *

When Dónal Lawler got back to his desk, he looked up the registration number of the red motorcycle he had seen parked beside the school in Nottingham Street. The bike did belong to Peter Ledwidge, as Karla had said. He had only owned it for a few months. It was a UK import, and with a little more digging, Lawler revealed that the machine had been bought from a dealer in Birmingham for just short of £4,000. Duty and VRT had been paid on it, and it had been given a contemporary Irish registration.

“Hmm... I wonder,” Lawler thought to himself. But his thoughts were interrupted by Burke who wanted to have a meeting of the team to discuss recent developments.

The detectives gathered around in the open plan area. Burke and Lawler brought them up to date with what had happened at the English school, and Burke went on to tell them about the phone call from Jude Kelly and said that the details of Darren Roberts' latest acquisition had been circulated.

"We need someone to go and interview Edith Walker. I'm sure it won't be long before a lawyer turns up for her, and as soon as he or she does, let's get things started," Burke said.

"What do you think is really going on there, boss?" Moore said.

"I can't be certain, but it looks as if Walker is either pimping out some of the students through the nightclub, or she's running a prostitution ring and the school is just a cover. While we're waiting for her lawyer to appear, why don't we do a little digging into whoever owns Ozone. See if we can make a connection to Walker. And I think it might be time to get Vice to pay a visit there next time they have a Spanish night."

Just then Amy Sutton came across and interrupted the meeting.

"I've just had control on, sir. Two Gardaí on patrol up in Rathmines have spotted Roberts' car. It's parked in the car park of the big Spar on the junction of Leinster Road and Rathmines Road. What do you want me to do, sir?"

"Tell them to keep watch and stay out of sight. Are they in a patrol car?"

"Yes, sir, an unmarked one."

"Excellent. C'mon, Fiona, let's go."

* * *

Once Burke and Moore were in Burke's car driving out of town towards Rathmines, Moore got on the radio to the two Gardaí who were watching Roberts' vehicle.

"What's the situation, please?" she said.

"We're parked in a laneway out of sight. We have eyes on the suspect's car, but there's been no sign of the occupant. What do you want us to do?"

"Stay put, but if there's any sign of him returning to the car, call it in, and if he takes off, follow at a discreet distance. OK?"

"Yes, Sarge, understood."

A few minutes later Burke pulled up across the entrance to the lane where the Gardaí were parked. He signalled for the female police officer sitting in the passenger seat to come across to his car. He wound down the window to speak to her.

"I want you to position your car just alongside the exit from the Spar car park. When chummy goes to leave, block his passage. We'll pull in behind him so he can't reverse out, and then we all hop out and grab the little toerag. Clear?"

"Yes, fine, sir. I'll just tell my colleague, and then we'll get sorted."

The Garda went back to her own car and sat in. Then Burke drove into the Spar car park just as the other unmarked Garda car got into the agreed position.

"What do we do now, boss?" Moore said.

"We wait, Sergeant, we just wait."

They didn't have to wait long.

The first they saw of Roberts was when he was opening the door of the old Polo and getting into it. He didn't hang around. The car started with a puff of blue smoke from the exhaust and started to move quickly towards the exit. Just as the nose of the VW was emerging from the car park, the unmarked Garda car pulled across in front of it, causing Roberts to summon whatever braking capacity his old wreck could manage and he pulled up just before he hit the Gardaí. Burke moved quickly, and positioned his own vehicle right up behind the rear of the Polo just as its reversing light came on, but Roberts could see he wasn't going to be able to drive off. He jumped from the car at the same time as the two Gardaí, as well as Burke and Moore, but he was quicker than all of them. He sprinted across the car park back towards the shop's entrance with the four police in pursuit. As he approached the door, he grabbed a couple of supermarket trollies and pushed them at the pursuers, but Moore dodged around and sprinted after him. Just as Roberts was about to enter the store, a woman pushing a buggy with two small children hanging out of it blocked his way, and Moore lunged at Roberts, felling him to the ground and landing on top of his back.

"Darren Roberts, I'm arresting you on suspicion of murder," and she went on to recite the remains of the arrest mantra as she placed his wrists behind his back and cuffed him. Roberts said nothing.

"Nice one, Fiona. Well done, everyone," Burke said. He turned to the female officer he had spoken to earlier. "Can you take this young man back into Store Street and book him in for us. I want to have a look in his car."

Chapter Twenty-Eight

Edith Walker had, as suspected, sourced a solicitor to look after her interests during the interview which would inevitably follow her removal from her place of work by the Gardaí.

The man's name was Eoin O'Rourke, and he came from one of the smarter legal practices housed in a large glass and brass office down along the South Quays, near Grand Canal Dock. He was very smartly dressed in a well-cut navy pinstripe suit, good leather shoes, a snow-white shirt and pale silk tie. Dónal Lawler guessed he was in his mid-forties, and did not look the type to be easily intimidated.

Lawler took a seat opposite the man and his client and explained that the interview would be recorded. He then recited the date, time and a list of those present.

"Mrs Walker, do you know why you are here?" Lawler said.

"No. I have no idea. I have done nothing wrong. This is outrageous, and I'm not without my connections, you know. You won't have heard the last of this."

Lawler was used to this kind of approach by suspects. It was a classic opening defence intended to put doubt into the mind of the Gardaí, but it was too well used to be of any value. Lawler had heard it all before.

"Mrs Walker, how is your business, The World of English, doing at the moment?" Lawler said.

The woman looked at her solicitor, who nodded imperceptibly.

"Very well, as it happens. We have good occupancy levels, and we are heavily booked going forward," Walker said. Then the solicitor put his hand on her arm, and narrowed his eyes, indicating to her that she should say no more on this particular topic.

"Yes, but are you actually making any money?" Lawler said.

At this, Eoin O'Rourke interrupted.

"Detective, I can't see that the business affairs of Mrs Walker's enterprise are any concern of yours. And it quite obviously has nothing to do with the current investigation. Indeed, it's difficult for me to see how you can possibly think Mrs Walker is in any way connected to the matter at all."

Lawler didn't acknowledge the interruption, but refocused his questioning all the same.

"Mrs Walker, we have received information that says your business is in financial difficulty. Is it not true to say that you have had to raise money through some rather curious, and may I say, unorthodox channels in the recent past to prevent it from going under?"

"That's preposterous!" Walker blurted, her face reddening as she spoke. "Who told you that? It's nonsense."

"In any case, so what?" O'Rourke intervened again. He was concerned that the Gardaí might have actual evidence of the loans to which Lawler had referred, and wanted to get off the topic as quickly as possible.

"I note that The World of English is not a limited company, Mrs Walker," Lawler went on. He was determined to keep the subject alive, but he was getting ready for a quick change of tack once he had the woman distracted.

"There's nothing wrong with that. It's perfectly legal," she said. She turned to her solicitor for confirmation, who nodded.

"Yes, it is. But it does mean that if it were to, say, go into liquidation, all of your personal assets would be made available to any creditors. You could lose everything you own."

"Look, officer, I have already told you that the school is in no danger of going bust. I don't know where you think you have got this information from, but it's inaccurate, and actually quite slanderous, so I'd ask you not to repeat any of it, is that understood?"

O'Rourke bowed his head and put his hand over his eyes. He would have much preferred it if his client left legal matters to him.

"What is your connection to the nightclub called Ozone, Mrs Walker?"

"What do you mean?" she said.

Classic delaying tactics, Lawler thought. She's giving herself time to think. She will be trying to figure out now just how much the Gardaí know.

"It's a perfectly straightforward question, Mrs Walker. Would you care to answer it?"

Walker looked again at O'Rourke who shook his head very slightly from side to side.

"No, officer, I wouldn't. I run a respectable business, and it's an English school, not a nightclub."

"But you obviously have some business with the place?" Lawler said.

Walker remained silent, but O'Rourke was back shielding his eyes again.

"What were you doing at the club when you were recorded on CCTV? What was your business there, Mrs Walker?"

"I... I was just looking in to see what kind of place it was. They have a poster on our noticeboard, and I wanted to see for myself what kind of establishment our students were going to. They run a Spanish night specifically to attract our lot. That's all."

"And are you a regular visitor to the club, Mrs Walker? And before you reply, remember we can check very easily."

"I may have been there once or twice previously, for the same purpose, you understand."

"I see," Lawler said. "But are you saying that you have no business relationship with the place? No commercial dealings with the club?"

"Of course I don't! What do you take me for?"

There was a knock at the door and Amy Sutton beckoned Dónal Lawler out of the room.

"Sorry to interrupt, but I thought you might like to see this. After Walker left Ozone the other day, she walked out onto O'Connell Street and went directly to the National Bank on the corner there. She deposited €1,000 in cash to the account of the school. Sorry we didn't have this earlier but the bank was being prissy about it."

"That's great, Amy, thanks."

Lawler went back into the interview room where Mrs Walker and Eoin O'Rourke were deep in whispered conversation.

"Now, Mrs Walker, just to be abundantly clear, you are saying that you have no business dealings or any commercial arrangements with Ozone of any kind. Is that correct?"

"Yes, I told you. Are you thick or something?" Walker said.

O'Rourke put his hand on his client's arm again intimating that she should restrain herself.

"I'm sorry, Detective. My client is finding this process very stressful. She's not used to dealing with law enforcement, and she is quite uncomfortable. Please forgive her rudeness. In any case, what exactly are you getting at?" O'Rourke said.

"Mrs Walker, may I ask if you often walk around the city streets with hundreds, maybe thousands, of euro in cash on your person?" Lawler said.

"Of course not. That would be stupid. Do I look stupid to you, Detective?"

"Then perhaps you can explain the fact that after you left Ozone the other day, you walked down onto O'Connell Bridge through the back lanes, along O'Connell Street and into the National Bank, where you deposited €1,000 in cash to the account of the school?"

Walker said nothing, but O'Rourke leaned over, and guarding his mouth with his hand, he whispered in Walker's ear. She then looked at Lawler triumphantly.

"That was fees, Detective. Many of our students pay their fees in cash, and of course it has to be lodged in full to the school's bank account which is held at the branch you mentioned."

"So, you didn't collect this money from Ozone, then?"

"Of course not. Why would they give me money?"

"Why, indeed!" Lawler said.

Lawler was careful not to mention, or hint at, what he considered to be prostitution going on at Ozone. Although it had been the basis for her arrest, they would keep that for another day. For now, he would have to let Walker go. Neither she nor her solicitor complained when he said she could leave. Neither of them was going to bring up the subject of prostitution, even though that's what had brought them there in the first place. They were just glad to be getting out.

But Lawler wasn't finished yet, and despite Mrs Walker's relief at getting out of the Garda station, she had an uneasy feeling developing in her gut.

Chapter Twenty-Nine

In another interview room further down the long corridor on the ground floor of Store Street Garda station, Darren Roberts waited for his interrogators to arrive.

Burke and Moore had decided that they would do the honours. They figured that the man was guilty of two murders, so they were in no humour to mess around. They were hoping that in an hour's time they would be in a position to charge him, and get him before a judge, when he would no doubt be remanded, as he was quite obviously a flight risk.

The two detectives bustled into the interview room, both carrying folders stuffed with papers. They took their seats before proceeding.

"Mr Roberts, you have been arrested on suspicion of involvement in the murder of two girls. I understand you have declined the services of a solicitor, is that correct?" Burke said.

"I ain't done nothing, have I? So, yeah, who needs a suit?"

Burke looked at Moore and raised an eyebrow.

"Very well. We will continue in that case, but I should remind you that these are serious charges, and if you change your mind at any point, please say so," Burke said.

"Look, mate, I told you, I ain't done nothing, so yeah, let's get on with it."

"Can you tell us what you are doing here, Mr Roberts?" Burke said.

"This bitch here jumped on me when I was doing me shopping, didn't she?" Roberts said. It seemed that every statement the man uttered had to be turned into a question.

"No. I mean what are you doing here, in Ireland?" Burke said.

"I'm on me holidays, aren't I? I believed the song, 'In Dublin's fair city, where the girls are so pretty,' so I thought I'd come over and see if it was true, didn't I?"

"And did you meet any pretty girls?" Moore said.

"Yeah, I did. But they were mostly Spanish prick-teasers, weren't they? Just my luck."

"What were the names of the girls that you met, Mr Roberts?" Moore said.

"Jesus, I don't know, do I? They was all foreign."

"Do you remember meeting a Gabriella, for example?" Burke asked.

"Might have done."

"Where exactly did you meet Gabriella then?"

"I dunno, do I? Some sleazy kip behind the river. A sort of a club thing. You want to see what they charge for drink in that place. It should be outlawed!"

"Where have you been staying, Mr Roberts?" Moore asked.

"Here and there. I stayed in that hostel place under the railway bridge just round the corner a few nights, didn't I?"

"Isaac's Hostel?"

"Yes, I think so."

"Tell me about meeting Gabriella, Darren," Moore said.

"Not much to tell, is there? I was in that dump having a drink and making some moves, you know. She was friendly and I bought her a few drinks. Cost me a bleeding fortune, didn't it? Then we went for a drive in my car, but she got all shy and wouldn't let me do nothing with her, would she?"

"So, what happened then?" Burke said.

"She got all prudish on me. Said she wasn't that type of girl. I was a bit riled up, wasn't I? So, I dumped her out of the car, and took off. That was it. Never saw her again."

"Where exactly was this, where you let her out of the car?" Moore said.

"I dunno, do I? Some place up near the canal. A nice quiet spot where we could get on with it without being seen, if you know what I mean," Roberts said, smirking.

"But that's not really what happened at all, is it, Darren? You followed her into one of the old buildings up there when she was trying to get away from you, didn't you? And then you strangled her, isn't that right?" Burke said.

"No, it bleeding ain't. Where are you getting this crap from? I told ya, I threw her out of the car and drove off. She was fine when I last saw her, wasn't she?"

"OK, Darren. Tell us about the car you were driving. Where did you get it?" Moore said.

"I bought it from that chancer in the lane up off the river, didn't I? Bleeding robber. The bloody thing went on fire. Nearly toasted me alive."

"So, you are saying you didn't set it on fire then?" Burke said.

"No, course not. Why would I after paying good money for it? I was just driving along and then 'whoosh', up she goes. I had to run for me life."

"Then how come we have CCTV evidence showing you buying a can of petrol for it just before it went up in smoke?" Moore said.

"Oh, yeah, that's right. I remember now, the petrol gauge was busted, and I didn't want to run out, so I got a spare gallon just in case."

Moore looked at Burke. This wasn't going well. Roberts seem to have perfectly plausible answers to all of their questions, and after all they had no forensics to tie him to the actual killings.

"Why didn't you just rent a car when you got here, Darren? You would have had a nearly new vehicle that would probably have been cheaper in the end," Moore said.

"Yeah, but I didn't have me license with me, did I? And the public transport in this town is rubbish."

"Would it not be more accurate to say that you don't actually have a valid driver's license, Darren?"

"Whatever," the man said.

"Tell us about the second Spanish girl, Darren," Moore said.

"What do you mean?"

"Well, did you meet any other Spanish girls? Did you go back to the club at all?" Burke asked.

"Not likely. Once bitten and all."

"So, what did you do after the Toyota burnt out? What did you do for transport after that?" Moore said.

"I went back to yer man in the yard. We had a good old row about how he stiffed me with the first car, I can tell you. Do you know what the cheeky bugger said to me? He told me to go to a car dealers if I wanted a more reliable transport. Anyway, he agreed to give me the old Hyundai for €50 in the end."

"And what happened to that?" Moore said.

"Dunno. It just stopped, didn't it?"

"And where was it when it 'just stopped', Darren?"

"I don't bleeding know. What do you think I am, Google Maps or something?"

"And were you on your own when the Hyundai broke down, Darren?"

"Yeah, 'fraid so."

Burke looked at Moore and signalled that they needed to have a chat in private.

"OK, Darren. We'll leave it at that for now, but we'll be detaining you here for the rest of the day at least, so don't think this is over, because it isn't. Not by a long chalk," Burke said.

When they got outside, Burke and Moore went up to Burke's office.

"What do you reckon, Fiona?"

"I don't know, boss. It's a pity we haven't any forensics to tie him to the actual killings. But even if we had a hair or something on him, he could argue that he picked that up when they were snogging. The kills were pretty clean too. No blood spatter or anything. But I'll get back onto the lab and see what they say. Maybe they'll be able to find something," Moore said.

"Yes, maybe. Look, Fiona, before you go, I just wanted to apologise to you for being a bit narky with you before. That complaint was weighing on my mind. The boss even suggested I might have to transfer to Cork of all places."

"Cripes. How's it all going, anyway?"

"I think it's blown over. GCOS have said there is no basis to pursue an enquiry as far as the evidence is concerned, so Heffernan seems happy enough. Let's keep our fingers crossed."

"Yes. Definitely. Catch you later."

Chapter Thirty

When Dónal Lawler had finished the interview with Mrs Walker and her smooth solicitor, he returned to his desk. He wasn't looking forward to telling Inspector Burke that he had managed to get exactly nothing from the woman to help them with these puzzling cases. As he sat there staring blankly at his PC screen, an idea came to him.

The Honda Deauville was not a popular bike in Ireland. The Gardaí had a good few of them, but apart from that, they never really found favour with the biking fraternity. Some nick-named the machine the 'dullville' for its lack of raw speed. Honda had designed the bike as a comfortable commuter, and its twin-cylinder V engine layout was never intended to deliver speed – they had plenty of other bikes that met that need. No, the Deauville was intended for comfortable, safe commuting on busy urban roads and did not therefore appeal very much to the usual tearaways that flogged performance machines around the suburbs of Dublin making a tremendous amount of noise and terrifying the residents.

He looked up his notes where he had recorded the registration number of the motorcycle parked at the side of The World of English. He then went onto Revenue's website, and searched for the transactions where the bike had been imported into the country. He found a copy of the invoice that Ledwidge had been given when he bought the machine, and made a note of the dealer's phone number.

He picked up the phone.

It was answered by a man with a distinct Midlands accent, who simply said, "Birmingham Bikes."

"Good morning. I wonder if I could speak to someone on sales, please?"

"Sales, service, cleaning, and everything else around here. That's me. Who's calling?"

"Oh, hi. My name is Detective Dónal Lawler from the police here in Dublin. I'm making enquiries about a red Honda Deauville that you sold to an Irish guy a few months back. It was going to be exported to Ireland. Do you remember it at all?"

"Don't tell me he's pranged it already? Hard to do on one of those, too."

"No, it's nothing like that. May I ask your name?"

"Dave. Dave Marsden. Yeah, I do recall that as it happens. He was a nice young lad. He'd researched the bikes on the net for ages and finally found us, and the bike here. I was glad to be rid of it, to be honest. Those Deauvilles can be very hard to shift. We took it in as a part-exchange against, let me see, oh yes, a Pan European. A much better proposition. So, what's the interest anyway?"

"Well sorry, Dave, this is a bit of detail you may not recall. You don't by any chance remember what tyres the bike was fitted with?"

"Ah, very good, sir. So, you know about the tendency of those to lose the backend if you drive them a bit hard, especially in the wet. Yes, we fitted a Bridgestone Battlax to the rear. I didn't fancy the guy coming back having come off and blaming me for his trouble. In any case the tyre that was on it was shot."

"I see. And you're quite sure about that, Dave?"

"Look, mate, when it comes to bikes, no one knows more than me. I've been at this business for nearly thirty years and I know every bike that passes through here like it was my own, so yes, I'm quite sure."

"Great, thanks very much, Dave. That's been more helpful than you'll ever know. Cheers."

"Oh, OK. Cheers." Dave hung up. He wondered what all that was about, but he was soon distracted by a new customer arriving at his premises.

* * *

Detective Inspector Burke brought the team together just after lunch. He was clearly frustrated that the earlier interviews had yielded nothing, or at least very little, to advance their case.

"Right, listen up, everyone. We need to get our finger out on these two killings. The Super is getting impatient, and frankly, so am I. We have that English twit downstairs still, and for my money, he's our man, but so far, we have no actual evidence to tie him to the two Spanish girls. He's admitted he knew Gabriella, slightly, but that's about it. So, Fiona, is there anything more from forensics that we can use?"

"No, boss, nothing yet anyway."

"Damn. OK, anyone got any ideas?"

Dónal Lawler didn't want to share the information he had received from the motorcycle dealer in Birmingham just yet. He wanted to talk to his sergeant, Fiona Moore, first. He was afraid Burke would make him look foolish in front of the rest of the team.

Amy Sutton spoke up.

"Sir, I think we need to set up a sting if we are going to flush out the school and the club."

"OK, Amy. What do you suggest?"

Sutton, feeling more confident that her idea had not been dismissed out of hand, went on.

"I think we need to get some marked money into that club. Then we can see if it turns up in Mrs Walker's lodgement. That would make the connection she's denying," Sutton said.

"Yes, but that wouldn't help with the prostitution aspect of things, would it, Amy? All it will show is that she's getting money from the place, and that's hardly a crime."

"No, sir, I guess you're right. Unless..."

"Unless what, Amy?"

Sutton looked around self-consciously.

"Well, if we could get some of the marked money into the hands of one of the girls. You know, the ones that are entertaining men upstairs in the club."

"Cripes! Are you suggesting one of us goes to the club and pays one of the Spanish students for sex, Amy?" Burke said.

Sutton shifted uncomfortably in her seat.

"Well, whoever it was wouldn't actually have to do anything. They could make some excuse after they had handed over the cash, and leave."

"Sounds very dodgy to me, Amy. Would it not just be better if we raided the place some Thursday when we know that the Spanish students will be there doing their stuff?" Burke said.

Moore, sensing Sutton's discomfort with the way the conversation was going, stepped in.

"I see what Amy is getting at, sir. If we just raided the place, then we would certainly be able to arrest some of the girls, and the owner of the place for operating a brothel, but it wouldn't tie Walker in, and I'm sure she is using the place as a cash machine to shore up the school."

"Do we know who owns the place anyway?" Lawler said.

"No. It doesn't appear on the CRO website, and Revenue have no information about it either," Moore said.

"Do you think you could set up what Amy is suggesting without it blowing up in our faces, Fiona?" Burke said.

"Probably. We'd need to involve someone from Vice, but I'd say we could arrange something. What do you think?"

"I think you'd better keep me out of it, that's what I think. I know nothing about it, OK? Then if it all goes tits up, I just might be able to step in and save your asses. Jesus! You women are a devious lot!" Burke said.

Moore looked at Sutton and smiled.

* * *

When the briefing was over, Lawler sidled up to Moore sitting at her desk and told her about the conversation he had had with Dave Marsden earlier.

"Do you think there's something in it, Dónal? Seems like a bit of a long shot to me."

"Yes, me too. But it's a coincidence, and we don't like coincidences, do we?"

"Hmm... I see what you mean. But you said that this Ledwidge guy is clean. He seems like such a decent bloke, unless my radar is letting me down badly. But tell you what, just to be sure, do a bit more digging quietly. Don't say anything to the boss. He has enough on his plate, but see if there's anything worth looking at, OK?"

"Yes, thanks, Sarge. Mum's the word."

Chapter Thirty-One

At the end of that day, the detectives had no new information from forensics that could tie Darren Roberts to the murder of the two Spaniards. Burke called Fiona Moore into his office.

"Come in, Fiona. Look, I need to talk about our tourist friend downstairs. What are we going to do with him?"

"Can't we hold onto him till tomorrow?" Moore said.

"Yes, but we won't be any further on tomorrow, will we?"

"Oh, right, I see what you mean. OK, so we have him on various motoring offenses, and we know he's wanted in the UK. We could just hand him over to the Brits. At least we'd know where he was for a few weeks in any case."

"Yeah, but if he's killed two young women on our patch, I'd prefer to have him for that. Look, can you get forensics to go back out to the site of the first murder? Get them to do a really thorough sweep of the place. Leave no stone unturned. There has to be something we've missed. This guy can't be that smart!"

"OK, I'll sort it. And as for your friend downstairs, we have no evidence, and he doesn't seem in the humour for a confession. Unless we could find a few more levers to pull. Scare the daylights out of him. What do you think?" Moore said.

"What have you in mind?"

Moore just grinned and left him to it.

* * *

Edith Walker was worried. She hadn't enjoyed being interviewed by the Gardaí, even though she had been well protected by her solicitor throughout. But it was obvious that the Gardaí knew more. She calculated that they were just biding their time until they had their evidence organised. She'd have to be careful, but she couldn't afford to stop the activity at Ozone. If she did, the college would have to close almost immediately. She decided to make a call.

"Hi, Larry, it's Edith."

She went on to describe the morning's events to the man who ran Ozone.

"What do you want to do?" he said when she had finished her story.

"There's not a lot we can do. Just be extra vigilant. Look out for anything out of the ordinary going on. How many girls are due in tonight?"

"I'm not completely sure, four or five, anyway. There'll be some of your crowd in for sure," Larry said.

"Do you think we should pause the operation for a while?" Walker said.

"It's up to you, but I'd rather not. I'm not sure we could even if we wanted to, and besides, I need the money."

"I know. So do I. OK. Let's keep going then, but be careful, won't you? But I don't want to come to the club to collect the takings. I think that camera down the lane may be able to see who's coming and going. Is there somewhere quiet we could meet instead?" Walker said.

"Don't worry about the cameras. I'll take care of them. Just come here as usual. I'll make sure you're not seen," Larry said.

"OK. I'll see you then."

* * *

After she had briefed the forensic team with her boss's wishes, Fiona Moore contacted Inspector Liam O'Higgins whom she had dealt with previously. He was a senior officer in what was referred to as the Organized Prostitution Investigation Unit of An Garda Síochána. It was as close as you could get to a Vice squad without actually using the word in the title. O'Higgins had been very successful in closing down a number of illegal operations in Dublin. It was a sordid business, often involving trafficked young women from eastern Europe and China who became essentially sex slaves when they ended up in Ireland having been promised good jobs by the gangmasters. Thanks to a change in the law these hapless girls were seen as victims themselves of late, and only the people behind the illicit trade, and to a lesser extent, their customers, were treated as lawbreakers.

"Hi, Inspector, it's Sergeant Fiona Moore here from Store Street. I was wondering if we could call on you for some assistance with a kind of amateur prostitution ring that is operating in the city centre?"

Moore went on to describe the goings-on at Ozone, and the possible connection to the school run by Mrs Walker.

"Interesting. That one hasn't come up on our radar so far, Fiona. But it's a clever scam having the legitimate business fronting the whole thing. Did you say that two of the young women had been murdered?" O'Higgins said.

"Yes, it looks like that. But we haven't got any real evidence to connect their deaths to the nightclub, or the school. Not yet anyway," Moore said.

"So, what's your plan, then?"

Moore outlined her plan. She hoped that O'Higgins would be able to provide a punter who could go into Ozone with some marked €20 notes and somehow get them into the hands of one of the girls.

"But I'm concerned that it will look like entrapment, Inspector. What do you think?" she said.

"We should be OK on that score, Fiona. There was a European Court of Human Rights case where a Dublin man was pleading entrapment over a drugs deal that was a sting, and the EU threw it out. It went right to the top, but the judgement was that it was a fair cop. So, we don't worry too much about that anymore. Thankfully, the interpretation is pretty relaxed in our favour. I'm more concerned about our man breaking the law by purchasing sex, but I guess if he makes an excuse and leaves before there's any physical contact with the lass, then he'll be OK. He'll be recording the procedure, naturally."

"Do you think you can handle it for us?"

"Yes, no problem. I have a couple of guys that will fit the bill nicely. Give me the details of the place and any other information you have and I'll get working on it. But just to be clear, if we manage to nab whoever is behind the operation, it's our collar. OK?"

"I suppose so. But there may be other charges related to the killings as the investigation progresses. I'd like to keep that part of the case here, if you don't mind?" Moore said.

"Yes, that's fine. When do you want this sting to take place?" O'Higgins said.

"Thursday night would be good. The club has a Spanish night then, and that's when it's most active."

"Fine. Let me go and set it up then. How are you going to retrieve the marked notes?" O'Higgins said.

"The woman calls to the nightclub on Friday to collect the spoils and walks to the bank on O'Connell Street where she lodges it. I'm hoping we can lift her along the way. We'll need your guy to identify the currency though."

"Yes, that's not a problem. Let me give you a call back when it's all arranged. Bye for now."

"Bye."

O'Higgins had no trouble recruiting a young man for the operation at Ozone. The Garda would be equipped with a couple of hundred euro in marked €20 notes. The markings would be invisible to the naked eye, but would show up discreetly under ultra-violet light. O'Higgins briefed the young man, and arrangements were made for him to receive a phone call soon after he went upstairs with his quarry, so that he could make his excuses and leave without having to participate in anything illegal. They figured the girl would be glad to get the money without having to perform in any case.

Chapter Thirty-Two

The next day, Dónal Lawler was busy doing a deep dive on Peter Ledwidge, the young guy from The World of English who taught classes and owned a nice red Honda Deauville. It was slow and painful work, but eventually it led him to a Detective Sergeant Brian Mulvihill who operated out of Terenure Garda Station. Lawler called the station and got through to the man almost immediately.

After he had introduced himself to Mulvihill, he went on, "I've come across your name in connection with a Peter Ledwidge, Brian. Do you remember him at all?"

"Ledwidge, Ledwidge, let me see. Oh, yes, I do indeed. A very interesting young man. Hang on, I think I might have a file here somewhere. It wasn't that long ago."

Lawler could hear the sound of a metal filing cabinet being opened, and files being moved about. Mulvihill was back on the line a few minutes later.

"Yes, here we are. He came to our attention a few years ago. He was at that fancy mixed-gender school that's halfway between Rathmines and Ranelagh. Apparently, he gave one of the girls a bit of a thumping. Something about her dumping him and him going off on one with jealousy," Mulvihill said.

"I see. Was he charged?" Lawler said.

"No. The girl's parents were diplomatic corps, and they didn't want to draw attention to themselves. And Ledwidge's father is pretty well to do, so I imagine some money may have changed hands, but it was never disclosed. No action was taken against the lad at all."

"Wow. How did you get involved?"

"The school called us in. They were pretty horrified that one of their little treasures was set upon. It happened on the school grounds, so they were just being thorough, I guess. They may have thought there'd be an insurance claim arising, so they wanted to do things by the book. Ledwidge was asked to leave afterwards, and he went somewhere else," Mulvihill said.

"Is the girl still around?"

"No. Her father was recalled soon afterwards. No connection. It's just these diplomatic types get shifted pretty frequently. I don't know where he was posted, but the whole thing blew over fairly quickly. Anyway, what's your interest?" Mulvihill said.

"I'll tell you in a minute, but first can you tell me if the girl that was assaulted was by any chance Spanish?"

"Cripes, yes she was. How the hell did you know that?"

Lawler went on to outline the case that they were dealing with, shortening the story so as not to bore the other Garda.

"Hmm... and do you think Ledwidge may have advanced his liking for beating up young Spaniards?" Mulvihill asked.

"Could be. Although we have no other evidence tying him to the murder of the girls. Not yet anyway. But what you've told me is very interesting. Thanks for that. Any chance you could send me a copy of your file?" Lawler said.

"Yes, sure. I'll get one of the uniformed lads to drop it down later when I've made a photocopy. Store Street, is it?"

"Yes, thanks. That's great. Bye."

When Lawler had finished talking to Mulvihill, he went and found Fiona Moore who was just getting herself a cup of coffee in the makeshift kitchenette at the back of the large open plan office.

"Hi, Dónal. What's up?"

Lawler filled Moore in on the conversation he had just had with Mulvihill.

"Do you want to tell the boss, Sarge?" Lawler said.

"No, not yet in any case. It's all a bit tenuous. But I tell you what, why don't I go and call on Mr Ledwidge? I'll try and meet him at his accommodation in Trinity on some pretext."

"OK, Sarge, but for Christ's sake, be careful," Lawler said.

"Don't worry, Dónal, I can look after myself."

But Lawler wasn't so sure.

* * *

Fiona Moore contacted Peter Ledwidge at The World of English. He had been in class when she called, so she spoke to Janet O'Sullivan who promised to get him to call back as soon as his class was finished. True to his word, Ledwidge telephoned Moore at a few minutes past eleven.

"Sergeant Moore, you were looking for me," he said.

"Yes, thanks for calling, Peter. Look, I need to talk to you again. Nothing heavy, just a few more questions to clear up. Are you around this evening?" Moore said.

"I can be. I'll be in the library in Trinity after six. Is that any good?"

"Yeah, sure. Where is your accommodation in the college? I think you said you were a scholar," Moore said.

"Yes, I have a room in the Rubrics, House 24 on the first floor, why?"

"Gosh, I've never been in that building. I understand it's one of the oldest on the campus. I'd love to see it. Could we meet there?" Moore said.

"Yes, I suppose so. Shall we say 6:30?"

"Perfect. See you then."

Lawler had overheard the conversation, and was quite uneasy about Moore meeting Ledwidge in his rooms, but said nothing.

* * *

Burke came out of his office with a determined expression on his face. He said to no one in particular, "What's happening out at the old factory? Are forensics there or what?"

Moore picked up the conversation.

"Yes, sir. They're going over the place again as you requested."

"Well, don't you think some of you should be out there with them? If they find anything, it could be days before we know it otherwise," Burke said.

"Yes, sir. Just on our way."

Moore collected Amy Sutton and they drove out to the site of the first murder in a marked squad car.

"God, the boss is a bit tense, isn't he, Sarge?" Sutton said as they sped along Gardiner Street towards Mountjoy Square.

"He has a lot on his mind, Amy."

"You mean that business with the Swedish pilot. Sure everyone knows about that. I hope it doesn't go anywhere, her appeal, I mean. It would be rotten if he was transferred or had to leave."

"Yes, well I think the less gossip there is about it the better, Amy. It's his business to sort out."

"Yeah, I know, but it's all over the station. Anyway, do you enjoy working with the inspector, Sarge?"

"He's a damn good cop. And despite his somewhat rugged approach to us sometimes, he'd always have your back if there was trouble. He's covered for me once or twice when he didn't have to. But he hates it when there's nothing happening. He thinks a lot of you, by the way," Moore said.

"Does he? Really? He never says anything."

"Look, Amy, if you're looking for a bunch of flowers every time you have a bright idea, you're in the wrong job. But both of us have seen you in action, and it's pretty good. I liked the way you captured the video footage in Ozone. And Burke was impressed too, even if he said nothing."

"That's good to know, Sarge. Anyway, here we are. God, it looks as if the entire forensic squad from the whole of Leinster is here!"

There was a total of five white 4x4s parked in various places around the site of the old factory, and it looked like there was at least a dozen officers combing the entire area, all dressed in white scene-of-crime suits.

Milo Turner was standing just outside the blue-and-white tape that had been erected to cordon off the area, with his black and white dog beside him on the grass.

"Why don't you go and see if you can find whoever is in charge, Amy, but try not to get in the way. I'm just going to have a word with Mr Turner here."

Sutton wandered off, and Moore could see her asking a couple of the white-suited officers for the person overseeing the operation. Moore walked over to where Milo Turner was standing.

"Hello, Milo. How have you been keeping?" she said. She reached down and patted the ever-appreciative dog, who responded by licking her hand.

"Ah, fair to middling, you know. Have you not finished messing about up here yet?"

"Not quite. But we should be finished later on today. Anything strange?"

"Not a bit of it, but the place doesn't feel the same since, well, you know. Mrs O'Brien got the priest to say a Mass for the poor young lass. But did I hear tell that there was another one as well?" Turner said.

"Yes, I'm afraid so. Spanish too, up near Dolphin's Barn."

"Have you not caught the blighter yet then?"

"The case is progressing, Mr Turner. That's why we are here today following enquiries."

Milo Turner said nothing. Moore got the feeling he was not impressed with the progress, or lack of it.

Moore saw Sutton coming towards her with one of the suited forensic officers and excused herself from Milo's company. She introduced herself to the officer and said, "Anything new at all?"

"We're focusing on footprints, Sergeant. There are at least fifteen sets in various places. Most have been quite well captured by the soft earth, so we are busy photographing them and taking casts of the clearer ones. Oh, and there is something else. You know where you saw the motorcycle tyre pattern and the impression from the side stand? Well, we had another good go around there and we found a couple of drops of what looks like engine oil in the grass just there. They're going back to the lab for analysis just for completeness."

"What could that do for us?" Moore said.

"If you had a bike that you thought might have been the one that stopped here, we might be able to match the oil to that machine. There are usually tiny metal fragments in engine oil that are very distinctive."

"I see," Moore said, "that all sounds very scientific. But thanks. Let me know if you get anything significant, won't you?"

"Yes, of course."

"OK, Amy, let's leave these good people to their painstaking work. I need to get back."

Chapter Thirty-Three

Moore walked around from Store Street Garda station to keep her rendezvous with Peter Ledwidge at his rooms in Trinity College. The Rubrics are the oldest existing buildings in Trinity College. They were built in the 1700s, and as the name suggests are of red brick construction over a timber frame. The Rubrics have a somewhat chequered history. In 1734, Edward Ford, a fellow of the College and son of the Archdeacon of Derry, got into a skirmish with a group of boisterous undergraduates. Standing in the window of his room in the Rubrics, remonstrating with the students to be quiet – they were, it seems, somewhat the worse for wear from drink – the poor man was shot several times in the body and head, and died a couple of hours later from his wounds.

The rooms are rented out to enthusiastic Americans during the summer when the students have gone home. These tourists are particularly enthralled by the story that the ghost of Edward Ford wanders around the outside of the building at dusk, but sightings have been few and far between.

Getting rooms in the building is considered to be an important status symbol for students, and the application process is arduous and time-consuming. But once you have been awarded your room, you are at liberty to enjoy the place, and the status that it bestows.

The Rubric building had been modernised in recent years. En-suite facilities had been installed, but this work was done carefully and tastefully so as not to upset the ambiance of the ancient building. Peter Ledwidge's room was 24-2 on the first floor of House 24.

Moore knocked on the old oak door, and a moment later, Ledwidge appeared. He was dressed casually, as before, and invited Moore in. The room was decorated in period style, with bare wooden floorboards painted with dark wood stain and covered here and there with woollen rugs, complete with tassels at their ends. A round mahogany pod table occupied one corner, and at the far end of the room beyond a well-filled set of bookshelves, a wide single bed, unmade, was lined up against the wall. On the other side of the room a shelf supported a modern microwave oven that looked incongruous in this setting, and beneath the shelf there was a modern white fridge that looked equally out of place.

"Come in, Sergeant, welcome to my humble abode," the young man said. He swept his arm low across his body to usher Moore inside, and indicated the only easy chair in the room for her to sit.

"Can I get you a glass of wine, Sergeant, or are you not allowed to drink on duty?"

"I'm not officially on duty, Peter," she said, "so yes, wine would be very nice, thank you."

Ledwidge fetched a glass and took an unopened bottle of chardonnay from the fridge, unscrewing the stopper and pouring a generous measure into a clean wine glass. He gave it to Moore, and raised his own glass in a mock toast.

"Cheers," he said.

They both took a sip of the cool, refreshing liquid.

"So, what is it you need to ask me, Sergeant?" Ledwidge said.

"Ah, it's nothing really. It's just about your motorbike. How long have you had it?"

"Just a few months. I had to save up for a long time to get it, but I've wanted one of those for ages."

"Where do you keep it?"

"The Dons of Trinity are not at all keen on motorcycles. They say they lower the tone of the place. But in an uncharacteristic concession they have provided a covered parking facility for us well out of sight down beside the Samuel Beckett Theatre. Of course, we are not allowed to actually ride the things on campus. We have to turn off the engine at the back gate and push the bikes along to the parking place."

"Where did you get it? There aren't that many of that particular type around. I know the Gardaí have a few, but apart from that, they are quite unusual," Moore said.

"I had to import it. It's no big deal. England has a plentiful supply of every kind of bike you could ever want, and they are normally very well kept. Why the interest, anyway?"

"It's something and nothing really. Just one of the witnesses said they thought they heard a motorbike taking off around the time that one of the Spanish girls was murdered. But they couldn't be certain, and they didn't actually see it or anything. So, we're just checking up on all the loose ends."

"I see. And how is the enquiry going? Have you any suspects yet?" Ledwidge said.

"I'm sorry, Peter, I can't discuss any of that with you just now. I'm sure you understand. But tell me, how long have you worked at The World of English?"

"It must be a couple of years now. It's handy money, and Mrs Walker is a sweetheart."

"Yes, she's very nice. Sorry, but is there any chance I could use your bathroom? This wine seems to have gone right through me."

"Yes, of course. It's the door opposite the bed, just there," he said. He pointed towards the only other dark brown door in the room.

Moore stood up and went into the bathroom closing the door behind her. She ran the cold tap gently, and opened the mirrored cabinet above the basin. She found what she was looking for immediately. She removed a small tuft of the man's hair from his hairbrush and put it in a small evidence bag she had in her pocket then closed the cabinet silently. Then she flushed the toilet, waited a moment or two, turned off the tap and came back into the room.

"Thanks. So, tell me, Peter, what hobbies do you enjoy?" She sat down again in the easy chair.

"I don't really have time for hobbies. I'm studying for a masters, and what with the teaching and everything, I'm more or less fully occupied all of the time."

Moore continued with the banal conversation for another twenty minutes. She declined another glass of wine, despite the young man's insistence, and then, saying that she had to get back to the station, got up and left.

When she was back outside, she made sure to exit the campus by Front Square and the main gate. She wanted Ledwidge to see her leave that way, if, as she suspected, he was watching her departure. But once outside on College Green she followed the railings of the College around into Pearse Street and slipped in under the barrier at one of the rear entrances to the College.

She found the motorbike park easily enough. There were five bikes in all parked under a rudimentary shelter that would keep the worst of the rain off the machines, but still allowed easy access to them. Ledwidge's red Honda was in the middle of the five. Moore had a good look around. There was no one about, and although she could see a camera positioned over the door of the nearby theatre, she felt sure that it was not able to capture her presence or her movements.

Moore donned vinyl gloves. She had studied the anatomy of the Honda Deauville on the web before leaving the station. She bent down and unscrewed the engine oil filler cap which doubled as a dipstick. Lifting it out carefully, she allowed several drops of the viscous liquid to drip into a sterile glass phial that she had brought with her. She repeated the exercise until there was about a third of a teaspoonful in the phial and then put the dipstick back in and screwed it home. She put the little bottle in her pocket and stood up. There was still no one around, so she left the way she had come and went back to the station.

When she got back to her desk, she labelled the phial of oil that she had taken from Ledwidge's Honda and set it on her desk. But she wasn't finished yet.

* * *

Michael Kelleher was two hours into his shift on his white cop bike when he got a radio message to attend Store Street Garda station as soon as possible and report to Detective Sergeant Fiona Moore.

He did as requested, and when he got to the station twenty minutes later, Moore came down to the front desk to meet him.

"Hi, Michael. Thanks for stopping by. Can I ask you, Michael, if you always use the same motorbike?"

"Yes, of course. Unless it's been crashed or something, but thankfully this one hasn't had any problems, so I've been paired with it for more than a year. Why?"

"I know you're going to think I'm completely bonkers, but humour me please. I need to get a few drops of engine oil from your bike in this glass bottle here. I don't need much. It won't affect the running of the bike at all."

"I see. OK. Can I ask what you want it for, Sergeant?"

"It's just for comparison purposes, Michael. Can we do it now?"

"I guess. But it will be quite hot. Better let me handle it."

"Fine, thanks."

The two of them went outside, and Kelleher took the little glass bottle from Moore, opened the filler cap on his bike, and dropped some hot oil into it from the end of the dipstick. He repeated the process twice and then turned to Moore and asked, "Is that enough?"

"Yes, perfect. Thanks very much, and sorry to have disturbed your shift."

"That's OK. But I'd better get back on the job. It's quite busy tonight."

As Moore labelled the second phial of motor oil back at her desk, she said to herself, "Magic. Oil and fingerprints too! Lovely!"

Chapter Thirty-Four

The atmosphere in Ozone was anything but fresh. Conor Duggan couldn't analyse the full range of smells that were assaulting his olfactory system, but none of it was entirely wholesome, that much he knew.

He went to the bar and ordered a Guinness 0.0, a new alcohol-free drink introduced by Diageo that looked exactly like the real thing and tasted good to boot. He heard other patrons calling the bartender Larry, so when he wanted a second pint of the harmless brew, he called him by name. It was as if they were old friends.

As Larry presented the young Garda with his fresh pint, Duggan said, "Any action in here tonight, Larry?"

"'tis a wee bit early yet, son, wait another while till the Spanish girls come in. Then you can have your pick."

"Cheers."

Half an hour went by, and Duggan was beginning to get a little impatient, when suddenly the atmosphere in the place changed radically. A group of six lovely-looking girls entered the club, chattering and giggling away in Spanish. They were dressed for a party and all looked fantastic as they made their way to the bar and kept Larry busy preparing drinks, most of which seemed to be either shorts or cocktails of one kind or another. Duggan noticed that no money changed hands.

Garda Conor Duggan was a good-looking young man of twenty-five years. He had a swarthy complexion, which meant that in the half light of Ozone, he could easily pass as a foreigner. At least, that is the impression that his appearance would leave with anyone on first acquaintance.

It wasn't long before a cute Spanish girl sidled up to him at the bar and engaged him in conversation. After a minute or two, she was already touching his arm and flirting outrageously with him, to the extent that he felt quite entitled to slip his arm around her bare midriff, to which she did not object in the slightest. He bought the girl a couple of drinks at very inflated prices, and after half an hour of meaningless chatter – 'Where do you come from? What are you studying? Do you like Dublin?' etc. – Duggan decided it was time to get down to business.

"Is there anywhere we could go that is a little more private?" he whispered in her ear.

His companion caught Larry's eye. Larry nodded slightly, and with that the girl took Duggan's hand and led him to a dark-coloured door over in the corner of the dancefloor. A minute later and the two of them were in a small, hot bedroom with subdued lighting. The room had no window, and the bright red and pink furnishings gave a strong clue as to the purpose of the room.

"Come here, my sweet," the girl said, wrapping her arms around his neck. "Now you know I have to charge you for my time with you, don't you?" she said seductively.

"Yes, of course. How much?"

"One hundred and fifty for an hour with full service. Is that OK?"

"Yes, fine."

Duggan peeled off the notes from a bundle of twenties and tens he had in his trouser pocket. The girl took the money, counted it and folded it before slipping it into a drawer beside the bed. Then she approached Duggan and started to remove his jacket. Just as she was getting around to loosening his tie, his phone rang.

"Sorry. I need to answer this," he said, retrieving his phone from the now discarded jacket which was over the back of the only chair in the room.

"Yes. Yes, this is Conor."

Duggan feigned alarm on his face as best he could as the caller spoke to him.

"God! Is she OK? What hospital have they taken her to?"

The caller recited some more of the pre-prepared text.

"OK, OK, I'll be there soon. This is terrible."

The Spanish girl asked him what was wrong when the call was over as he reached for his jacket to put it back on.

"I'm sorry. I have to go. My mother has collapsed at home and she has been taken away in an ambulance. I'm sorry. They need me immediately."

"Oh, I'm sorry, my sweet. I hope she'll be OK. But you must go to her. Maybe I'll see you again."

"Yes, maybe. Bye," he said. He left the building as quickly as he could.

Job done.

When he was well clear of the place, he telephoned Liam O'Higgins as arranged.

"Hi, Inspector. That's all been taken care of, sir. The girl's name is Alena, and she's studying English at The World of English, though to be honest, she doesn't need to. Her English is as good as mine," Duggan said.

"How much did she take off you?"

"She took €150, €140 in twenties and a single ten-euro note, all marked."

"Great. And you'd be able to identify her again?" O'Higgins said.

"Definitely, sir, no question."

"Good man. Well done. I'd better let Store Street know. Thanks."

"Goodnight, sir."

Inspector Liam O'Higgins called Detective Sergeant Fiona Moore.

When she answered, he said, "That little job you wanted has been attended to, Sergeant. We're all set for the morning then, yes?"

"Yes, fine, sir. Thanks for letting me know."

* * *

The following morning two groups of detectives organised themselves for a stake-out on Mrs Edith Walker. They had no idea when she would put in an appearance at Ozone, but they were fairly certain that she would, and they didn't want to miss her. If she followed her usual pattern, she wouldn't arrive until late morning but the Gardaí didn't want any slip-ups, so they got into position early.

There were very few places where they could conceal themselves along North Lotts, so they decided not to try. Where the lane met the busier thoroughfare of the quays, there was a coffee shop on the corner, so Amy Sutton and one of Liam O'Higgins' men positioned themselves there. They had a map of Dublin spread out in front of them to make it look as if they were tourists.

Out on O'Connell Street, Lawler and another of O'Higgins' men were seated outside a similar coffee shop which had spread itself out onto the pavement. Moore was mobile. She was walking around between the bank on O'Connell Street along the route that Walker was known to use, and the club, but doing so in a way that meant she wouldn't be recognised. Unfortunately, the CCTV camera that should have recorded Walker entering and leaving Ozone wasn't working, and they didn't want to send out a crew to repair it for fear of spooking anyone.

Burke was back at the station with Liam O'Higgins co-ordinating the stake-out, keeping closely in touch with the teams by radio.

The morning went in slowly enough

At just after eleven o'clock, Moore was walking briskly along North Lotts at the far end from the club when she spotted Mrs Walker going into the premises. She quickly turned her back on the place and hit the transmit button on her radio.

"Stand by, everyone. Suspect has been seen entering Ozone. I expect she will be back out again in a few minutes. I will try and maintain surveillance and give you notice if she's coming your way."

The next fifteen minutes crawled by.

Then, Edith Walker emerged from Ozone, but she wasn't on her own. Larry the barman was with her, and they were having what looked from afar to be a heated argument. Larry pushed the woman, and she staggered back, but managed to keep her footing. Then she turned and ran towards the end of the lane. Larry just threw his hands up to heaven and cursed out loud. He didn't pursue her.

Moore was back on the radio.

"Amy, she's headed your way. Please detain her, and make sure she doesn't dispose of anything anywhere. There's a car waiting on Middle Abbey Street that can be with you in two minutes."

"Thanks, boss. Don't worry, we'll get her."

Mrs Walker came around the corner onto the quays glancing furtively behind her and looking very flustered. On cue, Amy Sutton and her companion sprang up from the table at which they were sitting, and each of them grabbed one of Walker's arms. While O'Higgins' man read her the arrest mantra, Sutton got on the radio again.

"Suspect detained. Please send the car to the corner of North Lotts and the quays."

When Mrs Walker had been bundled into the back seat of the squad car, protesting loudly, Sutton radioed in again to advise everyone that their mission had been accomplished. Burke came on the air.

“Well done, everyone. Clear to stand down. Fiona, Amy, Dónal, please return to the station. Thanks, everyone.”

Chapter Thirty-Five

The Gardaí now had two suspects in custody, although no one thought that Mrs Walker could have actually murdered either of the Spanish girls. But she was certainly up to no good.

When Moore and Sutton got back to the station, Burke called them into his office.

"How did that go?" he said.

"Pretty good, thanks, boss. O'Higgins has taken her away to get her booked in and no doubt await the arrival of her lawyer. She wasn't happy, but she had a decent amount of cash on her, and it won't take us long to confirm that it includes some or all of the notes Duggan handed over to the girl in the club."

"OK, Fiona. Look, I want you to stay with that, if you don't mind. I don't want O'Higgins bagging all the glory. It was our lot that discovered the whole thing for starters, and I'm still not convinced that there isn't a connection to the murdered girls. So, stick close, and see if we can get to interview her on our own before she gets bailed, or whatever."

"Boss, can I have a word, in private?" Moore said.

"Sure. Thanks, Amy. That's all for now. Good work."

Amy Sutton left the inspector's office wondering what it was that her sergeant wanted to talk to the inspector about in private. What else was going on that she didn't know about?

Moore filled her boss in on the evidence she had collected from the two Honda Deauville motorbikes.

"I've sent the two samples up to The Park for analysis, and comparison with the trace that they found out along the canal near Milo Turner's house. They should be able to get back to me later on."

"Do you not think this is all a bit far-fetched, Fiona? I mean we have Walker in custody now, and for my money, I bet she'll tell us most of the story once we put a bit of pressure on her. She's looking at a very serious charge if she has been pimping out her students after all."

"Maybe. But I'd just like to see this through, sir. It may have something to do with whoever damaged my car, as well."

"OK. If you insist. But don't spend too much time on it. We have Darren Roberts to deal with too, don't forget," Burke said.

"Yes, I know. What exactly are we going to do with him?"

"I'm not sure. We haven't really got anything definitive on him, except a few minor motoring offences. But there is some connection to the dead girls, I'm sure of it. I have a feeling he may be a bit more involved than it looks. Anyway, we can hang onto him till later this evening, and I could probably get an extension if it comes to it. Let's see what the rest of the day brings."

"OK, boss. I'd better go and see how O'Higgins is getting on with Mrs Walker."

"Fine. Catch you later."

* * *

Fiona Moore went and found Inspector Liam O'Higgins who was just finishing a cup of coffee and a biscuit in the open plan area of Store Street Garda station.

"Hi, Inspector. What's the story?" Moore said.

"Walker's lawyer has arrived. I'm going down to question her now. Would you like to sit in?"

"Yes, please. But I'll let you lead, OK?"

"Yes, please. Let's go," he said. He drained the remains of his drink and put the mug down on the nearest desk.

As soon as they entered the interview room where Edith Walker and her solicitor, Eoin O'Rourke, were seated, the lawyer started to protest. O'Higgins had come across the man before, so he knew the form. He let O'Rourke have a rant for a few minutes, wittering on about police harassment, human rights and all the other guff he could come up with.

When O'Rourke seemed to have temporarily exhausted himself, O'Higgins spoke.

"Well, now that we've got all that nonsense out of the way, perhaps we can get down to actually questioning your client about her illegal activity."

"And I assume you have evidence of that allegation, Inspector," O'Rourke said.

"Last night, one of our undercover operatives went to Club Ozone where he made friends with a young Spanish girl called Alena. Alena is currently attending Mrs Walker's college of English as a student," O'Higgins said.

"So what? It's hardly a crime, is it? And that place has a special night for the Spanish on Thursday, so it's only natural that she would be there with her friends. I'm afraid you'll have to do better than that, Inspector," O'Rourke said smugly.

"Yes, and I can," O'Higgins replied. "Alena offered sexual favours to our man, and took €150 from him in payment for same. Naturally, our undercover officer made his excuses and left before anything untoward took place."

"I can't be responsible for what my students get up to when they are not in college, Inspector. I'm not their mother, you know!" Walker said.

"Ah, yes, indeed. And, strangely, it's not illegal these days for young women to sell their services. But you see there's more. The notes that our man handed to the girl were marked. And quite a large amount of the marked notes were found on your person, Mrs Walker, when you were detained earlier. How do you explain that?"

"Mrs Walker has an arrangement with Ozone, Inspector. She allows them to promote the club at The World of English, and they pay her a small fee. There's nothing illegal in that, now is there?" O'Rourke said.

"A small fee, you say. Mr O'Rourke, we have looked into Mrs Walker's bank account, and it shows that your client lodges over €1,000 every Friday in cash after she has visited Ozone. That seems to be a very large amount of money just for allowing them to promote their venue at the college."

Neither O'Rourke nor his client said anything.

"So, maybe you'd like to tell me the real reason that Ozone pay you so much money every week on the day following their Spanish night?" O'Higgins said.

"No comment," came the reply.

"I see. Well, let me tell you what I think then. I think you're pimping out some of your students in the club on Thursdays and taking a good slice of the money that they earn selling sex. Isn't that what's happening, Mrs Walker?" O'Higgins said.

"That's preposterous. You have no proof whatsoever, and that's a very serious allegation, Inspector," Walker said. She had gone quite red in the face.

"Isn't it true, Mrs Walker, that The World of English is in financial difficulty?" the inspector said.

"Who told you that then? It's nonsense!" Walker replied.

"Is it, really? Perhaps you could tell me why you found it necessary to borrow €15,000 from Janet O'Sullivan to keep the college afloat?"

Walker went pale at this news. She had been betrayed by the person that she trusted implicitly with all her secrets. O'Sullivan had turned on her, after all she had done for the woman. This was the last straw.

"Well?" O'Higgins pressed on.

"No comment."

"So, we have established that the school is in trouble for money. We've established that you are in receipt of money paid to your students who are selling their bodies in the nightclub. You see, Mrs Walker, two and two still make four."

Fiona Moore excused herself from the interview. She had an idea.

Chapter Thirty-Six

When Moore had left the interview that O'Higgins was conducting with Mrs Walker, she went back upstairs. She found Amy Sutton and Dónal Lawler in the open plan chatting about the case.

"Amy, Dónal, I'd like you to drive around to The World of English and see if you can find a Spanish student by the name of Alena there. If you find her, bring her in. Don't say anything at all to her, just get her to come in to the station and when you have her, let me know."

"OK, Sarge. That's all a bit mysterious. What's the craic?" Lawler said.

"I'll tell you later. Just go and get her, will you?"

"On our way," Lawler said, looking sideways at Sutton.

* * *

Half an hour later, Alena Sanchez was seated rather uncomfortably in an interview room in Store Street Garda station. She was a pretty girl, with long dark hair and a very trim figure, nicely contained in well-fitting blue jeans and a snug woollen jumper.

Moore went into the interview room and introduced herself.

"Thanks for coming in, Alena. Look, I just want to say that you're not in any trouble. Well, not really anyway. I just need some information from you, OK?"

"What are you going to do to me?" the girl said, nervously.

"Nothing. Nothing at all. I just need you to help me with something, that's all."

Sanchez still didn't look comfortable, but relaxed a little when she heard what Moore had to say.

"Alena, last night a man came to Ozone and you went upstairs with him. He gave you some money and I think we both know why that was, don't we?"

"Oh my God. Was he a policeman?" Alena said.

"Yes, yes he was. But please don't worry. You may be able to help us, in which case we may not need to bring charges. Are you willing to help?"

Alena teared up.

"Do my parents have to find out?" she said.

"No, of course not. At least I don't think so. What age are you?" Moore said.

"Nineteen. I have my ID card here. You can see," Alena said. She rummaged in her small handbag and produced the card which confirmed that she was indeed nineteen years old.

"In Spain, it is not illegal, what we were doing, you know. I think it is the same here," Sanchez said.

Moore was a little taken aback by the girl's knowledge of the business.

"So, tell me, Alena, how did you get into all this?"

"There is a group on Facebook that we are all in together. Several girls from my city belong to it. The lady who runs the English school is in it too, and she invites us to come to Dublin where we can get a lot more money for what we do. I get to keep half of what I earn, so it is good money."

"I see. And have you any messages on your phone or computer that would help us to prove what you are saying, Alena?"

"Yes. I have messages and emails. I can give them to you if you agree not to prosecute me, and not to tell my parents. They would be very sad at what I am doing."

"OK, well how about you give me your phone and show me how to get the messages, and then someone will take you upstairs and you can log onto your email account here. Is that OK?" Moore said.

"Yes, I suppose. But what will happen about it?"

"You don't need to worry about that, Alena. But I think you should make plans to return to Spain. I think The World of English may be closing down soon. Can you give me the names of the other girls that are doing this too? And have you any information about the two students that were murdered?"

"God, that was awful. It really frightened us. Some of the girls ran away as soon as we heard about it. But Mrs Walker said it had nothing to do with the school or the club, and that we could continue. She would keep us safe," Sanchez said.

"And were you happy with that?"

"Not completely, but I needed the money. My younger brother is very sick at home, and needs operations that aren't covered by the government. My parents are poor, so I am saving up to pay for him at the hospital. It will cost more than €10,000, but he will be fixed."

"I see. Can I ask, Alena, how did you first come in contact with this group?"

"A friend told me about it. They said Dublin was a good place, and if we came to the school we would get the extra work in the club. It was going well. I have quite a lot saved now."

Moore couldn't help but feel sorry for the girl. She had no idea how prostitution worked in Spain, but she guessed it was pretty sleazy, and probably quite dangerous for the women involved. Mind you, she thought, Dublin hasn't turned out much better for two of them at least.

* * *

O'Higgins was taking a break from the interview with Edith Walker and her tireless advocate. He hadn't got much further, and was contemplating calling it a day until tomorrow, but knew that if he did so, he would have to release Walker on police bail pending further enquiries, and he didn't fancy that as a course of action.

"There you are, Inspector," Moore said when she joined him in the open plan. She went on to tell him about the information that she had received from Alena Sanchez.

"She's given us access to her emails. Pretty damning stuff, from what I can see. And she's writing out a statement now. I think it will give you enough to charge Walker, but I'll leave that up to you."

"That's great news, Fiona. Thanks for your help. I wasn't really getting anywhere with herself and that pesky solicitor of hers. He's a real smoothy."

"Yes, I know the type. Anyway, give us another half an hour and then you should be good to go. Excuse me, I have something to do."

* * *

Moore saw that Aidan Burke's office was empty, so she went in and closed the door. She called Keith in the technical bureau from the phone on Burke's desk.

"Hi, Keith, it's Sergeant Moore. I was just wondering if you have any news on those oil samples I sent you up earlier?"

"Oh, yes, I have as it happens. Interesting. The one that you labelled 'Kelleher' has nothing to do with anything. It doesn't match the trace we found in the grass. But the other sample is more interesting for two reasons. Firstly, it is a match for the drops that were taken from the path outside the place where the first girl was killed. Same brand in any case, and we're fairly certain it's from the same engine. We have some more tests to do, but it's a ninety percent fit as it is. And there's more. That oil isn't your usual common or garden stuff you find at the local petrol station. It's a specialist product, Honda Pro GN4. I don't think it's available in this country."

"Wow! I see. And that's the stuff from the sample I marked as 'Ledwidge'. Is that right, Keith?"

"Yep! That's it."

"Excellent. I have one more phone call just to make sure, but that sounds very positive. Can you write it all up for me?"

"Yeah, but not till tomorrow if that's OK?"

"Sure. Tomorrow is fine. Thanks."

Moore went and found Dónal Lawler.

"Dónal, did you speak to the dealer that Ledwidge bought his motorbike from?" Moore said.

"Yes, I did. Dave was his name, Marsden, I think."

"Great. Have you got his phone number handy?"

"Hang on. It's here somewhere."

Lawler rooted around amongst the papers that were on his desk.

"Yeah, here you go. Do you want me to call him again?"

"Yes please. Ask him what brand of engine oil he put into Ledwidge's bike before he delivered it to him. I bet he did an oil change on it before it went out."

Lawler made the call. Moore could only hear one side of the conversation, but as it went on, Lawler wrote down 'Honda Pro GN4' on his jotter. Moore smiled to herself.

Chapter Thirty-Seven

Moore called Burke on his mobile phone and told him about the motorbikes.

"Christ! Does that mean that this Ledwidge guy is our man for the murders?"

"Well, that's a bit of a leap. But we now know that his bike was the one that stopped up at the old factory where we found Gabriella's body. He certainly has some questions to answer."

"Are you sure about this, Fiona? If we go off half-cocked and bring him in, it could go very badly for us," Burke said.

"The forensics are pretty conclusive, sir. It's not just the oil. We have the tyre pattern matched as well, and I'll wager that if we lift Ledwidge's bike, we'll find small traces of mud from at least one of the sites too," Moore said.

"OK. Well, we better make sure we do this right. We need to lift him first. Then we can legitimately grab the bike and hand it over to forensics. I'd say early doors tomorrow, wouldn't you? We don't want to make a big fuss in Trinity when the place is thronged with tourists. The Provost wouldn't appreciate that. If we go in at around 5:00 a.m., the place will be empty and the students will all be asleep. Set it up then. Get a few plain clothes Gardaí to help out, and can you handle it with Dónal?" Burke said.

"What! Another night of beauty sleep bites the dust! Yes, of course. No problem," Moore said.

* * *

Moore and Lawler met in the car park of Store Street Garda station at four forty-five the following morning. The plan was to go in the back entrance of the College and approach the Rubrics from behind. They would position two plain clothes Gardaí at the rear of the building, while Moore and Lawler would adopt a frontal approach up the main stairs. They hoped to find Peter Ledwidge asleep in his bed, hopefully on his own, and take him into custody with the minimum of fuss. How wrong they were.

Peter Ledwidge had been at a party that night, and had only just arrived back to his room when the Gardaí approached. He was a little bit drunk, but not incapacitated, and he saw Moore and Lawler enter the Rubrics building quite clearly from the window of his own room. He knew there was only one staircase that served the building, but for safety reasons, Trinity had installed special ladders at the end of the corridor. These were fixed to an internal wall, and were deployed by unfolding them and throwing them out through the window under which they were anchored. In this way they made a kind of flexible ladder with wooden rungs that could be used for escape in the event of fire.

Ledwidge grabbed his wallet and phone and ran out onto the corridor. He sprinted to the end and quickly undid the ladder, chucking it out the window and nimbly climbing out, descending to the gravel below just as Moore and Lawler arrived at his door, which, in the rush to escape, he had left open.

Moore was quick to react. She went to a window at the back of the building and shouted to the plain clothes men beneath.

"Quick. Get after him. He's headed for the Beckett Theatre to get his bike. Don't let him get away!"

The two Gardaí dashed off towards the back gate where Ledwidge's bike was tethered. They caught up with him as he fumbled with his keys to undo the stout ABUS lock and chain that was wrapped around the front wheel of the machine and the stanchion that was cemented into the ground securing it.

When Ledwidge saw the two men approaching, he threw his keys at them and took off on foot. But the young Gardaí were fit, and Ledwidge was just a little unsteady on his feet, and as he ducked down to go under the barrier that would get him out onto Pearse Street, he stumbled and fell. The two men were on him at once, and within seconds had him handcuffed and restrained.

* * *

Ledwidge was brought back to Store Street and booked in with the night man. Moore had stayed behind at Trinity to smooth over the whole affair with the College authorities who had become aware of the melee despite the early hour.

Lawler had gone back to Store Street with the prisoner and accompanied him as he was booked in with the night sergeant, having been arrested on suspicion of murder. Lawler decided that he would allow Ledwidge a few hours' sleep before starting to question him in the company, no doubt, of the duty solicitor.

It was ten o'clock when Moore and Lawler commenced the interview with Peter Ledwidge. Surprisingly, the young man had declined the services of a solicitor, saying that as he had done nothing wrong, he didn't need one.

"If you change your mind at any time during this interview, Peter, all you have to do is say so, and a solicitor will be provided," Moore said as she sat down opposite the suspect clutching a takeaway coffee.

"What happened your face?" Moore asked.

Ledwidge instinctively put his hand to his cheek.

"Oh, that. It's nothing. I fell out of bed and scratched it, that's all."

Ledwidge presented an arrogant demeanour, quite possibly encouraged by the residual alcohol that was still in his system from the night before.

"What's all this about, anyway?" he said, challenging Moore.

"Tell me about your relationship with Gabriella Ortez, Peter," Moore said.

"There's not much to tell. We went out together a few times, that's all. Then I gave up on her when I discovered she was a slut."

"How do you mean?" Lawler said.

"Well, I'm sure you know what's been going on at that dump Ozone. You are supposed to be detectives, after all."

"And what exactly would that be, Peter?"

"Bloody hell. It's a knocking shop. Those wide-eyed and innocent Spanish chicks are on the game, aren't they?"

"Are they? Do you have any actual evidence of that at all?" Moore said.

"I dunno. That's your job. I'm just a teacher."

"How many of the Spanish girls have you been going out with, Peter?" Moore said.

"A few."

"Names?" Moore said.

"I dunno. They all have weird names anyway."

"How long were you dating Alicia Navarro?"

"I told you before, we went out a few times. So what?"

"So what, is that she was the second girl to be murdered from The World of English in similar circumstances."

Dónal Lawler, sensing that they weren't really getting anywhere, changed tack.

"Tell me, Peter, how long have you had your Honda?"

"What's that got to do with anything?" the young man said.

"Just answer the question please," Lawler said.

"A few months. Why? Are you thinking of getting one?"

"And have you had it serviced since you got it?"

"No. It doesn't need it. The dealer I bought it from gave it a good service before I collected it, didn't he?"

"Tell us about the last time you saw Gabriella, Peter," Moore asked.

"It would have been at the school. She was in one of my classes, but I can't remember the date. Maybe a couple of weeks ago."

Moore decided to turn up the heat.

"Peter, have you ever parked your bike along the canal?"

"No. Why would I do that?"

"Peter, we have evidence that places your motorcycle on the path alongside the old factory where the body of Gabriella Ortez was found."

"That's nonsense. What evidence?"

"Conclusive forensic evidence, Peter," Lawler said.

"Nah. You're bluffing. And now, I think I'd like to have a solicitor."

Chapter Thirty-Eight

While Moore was waiting for Ledwidge's solicitor to arrive, she went back upstairs. She felt the need to update Burke on their progress, such as it was. She found him in his office.

"Ah, there you are. Our English friend downstairs is kicking off. He says he wants to see us," Burke said before Moore could get a chance to tell him about the interview with Peter Ledwidge.

"What does he want?" Moore said.

"Who knows. But maybe we should go and see."

"OK. Ledwidge has called for a lawyer, so it will be half an hour or so before he's ready for more in any case."

When they got downstairs, the desk sergeant arranged for Darren Roberts to be brought to an interview room. When he arrived, he was clearly quite agitated.

Once they were all seated, Burke asked the man, "So, what do you want now, Darren?"

"I need to get out of here. It's doing me head in. I'll bugger off back to England and you won't see me again, promise."

"I'm afraid it's not that simple, Darren. There are some fairly serious charges facing you, and we don't know yet to what extent you were involved in the murder of the two young women," Burke said.

"Look, if I give you something on that, will you let me go?"

"That depends. If you have any information, you're duty-bound to share it. What do you want to tell us?"

"Well, it's like this. A couple of weeks ago I was in that Ozone place. I went to see if I could snag one of the students for a bit of... well, you know."

"Go on," Moore said.

"Well, I was having a drink at the bar, eyeing up the talent, when this big, tall gangly bloke came across and started talking to me. We chatted for a while, and then he asked me if I was up for a bit of a caper with one of the girls. I wasn't quite sure what to make of it, but I wanted to hear what he had to say. Anyway, to make a long story short, he told me to get with this Spanish tart – Gabriella her name was. He said he wanted to play a joke on her. I was to be all palsy-walsy with her, and take her for a drive in me car. I was to bring her up to this place along the canal, then pick a fight with her and chuck her out. That was it. Nothing more."

"What, just leave her there on her own?" Burke said.

"Yeah, that's it. You got it," Roberts said.

"I see. Very gallant, I'm sure. But wait. What was in it for you?"

"The bloke said he'd leave €50 behind the bar for me if I'd go along with it. It was just some prank he wanted to pull. Seemed harmless enough to me."

"So, did you do as he asked?" Moore said.

"Yes, I did. It wasn't hard to persuade her to come for a drive with me, and it was even easier to pick a fight with her. She was right feisty. So, I ditched her where he said, and took off."

"Did you get this bloke's name?" Burke said.

"He said his name was Peter something or other. I don't remember the rest of it. Then when I heard about the girl being killed, I torched the car the next day in case there was any trace left in it."

"So, when you told us that it had just caught fire, you were lying, Darren?" Moore said.

"Yeah. I guess. But it wasn't much of a lie."

Burke and Moore exchanged slightly exasperated glances.

"Would you recognise this Peter bloke again if you saw him, Darren?" Burke asked.

"Yeah, I guess so. He was tall, with a mop of fair curly hair, and thin. Do you think it was him that offed the girls?"

"That's still under investigation," Moore said.

"Now, can I get out of here?" Roberts said.

"Not so fast, matey. First, we'll need you to positively identify the man you said was willing to pay you €50 to lure the girl away. Then we'll have to check that he did in fact leave the money behind the bar in Ozone. After that, we'll see what the superintendent wants to do with you. Wait here."

Burke and Moore got up and left the young man in the interview room, instructing the sergeant at the desk to keep a sharp eye on him.

On the way back upstairs, Burke said, "Can you organise an ID parade? You can use a few of our own lads, and see if you can find someone that looks a bit like Ledwidge. But not too much like him. OK?"

"Yes, no problem, boss. I think if we had that along with the forensic evidence, he'd be banged to rights, don't you?" Moore said.

"Don't count your chickens, Fiona. There's many a slip, you know. But it's looking a bit better. When you go back in, ask Ledwidge if he would be prepared to participate in an ID parade. Oh, and get back onto forensics too. See if they have any more good news for us."

* * *

Moore called Keith in the forensic laboratory and asked him if he had any further evidence from either of the bodies or from the crime scenes that could help them.

"I have as it happens. You remember you brought me some hair from Ledwidge's hairbrush? Well, it matched the hair that we found in the second girl's fist. Of course, it's not entirely conclusive, but it may help."

"I think it definitely will, Keith. Thanks. Can you email me across the details?"

She then went back downstairs to continue the interview with Peter Ledwidge, now in the company of the duty solicitor.

When she had recited the necessary details for the recording device, Moore took a long look at the man that had been provided to Ledwidge to safeguard his interest. He was in his forties, overweight, poorly dressed and obviously very bored with the entire procedure. But Moore had seen something similar before, and was not convinced that based on appearance alone, he might not be quite a terrier when it came to defending his client.

"Now, Mr Ledwidge, can I ask you if you would be prepared to take part in an identity parade?"

Before Ledwidge could reply, the solicitor spoke up.

"Do you mean to say you have a witness to something that may or may not have taken place, Sergeant?"

"That's the usual reason for an ID parade, is it not?" she scowled at the man.

"Who is this witness? I've already told you I go to Ozone sometimes. The barman will have seen me there a few times."

"I'll ask again, Mr Ledwidge, are you happy to take part in an ID parade?"

Ledwidge looked at his brief who shook his head slightly.

"Yes, OK. I have nothing to hide."

The solicitor shaded his eyes with his hand.

"Thank you. Please wait here until I make the arrangements. It will take half an hour or so."

Moore left the room and went to find Burke to tell him the good news.

Chapter Thirty-Nine

Unsurprisingly, Darren Roberts identified with some certainty that Peter Ledwidge was the man who had put him up to the 'caper' with Gabriella Ortez. Ledwidge couldn't see Roberts through the one-way glass that separated the witness from the six people lined up in the brightly lit room, but on the way back to their various quarters, he caught a glimpse of the Englishman, and was clearly shocked to see him.

Moore and Burke wasted no time in getting back in with Ledwidge.

"Well, Mr Ledwidge, you have now been identified as the man who asked Darren Roberts to drive Gabriella Ortez to the site near where her body was found. Traces from your motorcycle have been found at the same site, and we have a DNA match from your hair with some hair found in the fist of Alicia Navarro which must have been pulled out when you were attacking her. I must tell you this is very serious for you. I will later be charging you with two counts of murder, but first I'd like you to answer some more questions for me."

Ledwidge was destroyed. He had gone ghostly pale, and was finding it difficult to speak. After a few moments of silence, he finally said, "He told me he was going back to England. He promised."

"That would be Darren Roberts that you're talking about then?" Moore said.

"What? Oh, yes. The guy from the club."

"Mr Roberts has been very helpful to us with our enquiries. He told us that you paid him to lure Gabriella to that place up along the canal where you strangled her. But what about Alicia, Peter?"

"That was easy. She was man-mad, and wild with it. She told me she wanted a go on my motorbike, so I took her for a ride out near Dolphin's Barn."

"But why did you come to us and report her missing then?" Moore said.

"To divert attention away from me, of course."

"But why did you kill these girls, Peter? What had they ever done to you?" Burke said.

"They made fun of me. Gabriella said she loved me, but then I found out she was going with men in that bloody club. It disgusted me. I couldn't have that. I have my pride, you know."

"And what about Alicia?"

"I was very fond of her. She had something about her. I don't know, but she was special. Then when we stopped along the canal to go and get something to eat, she started making fun of me. Called me names. I don't know. Perhaps she was just joking to get a rise out of me. She was very flirty. But I just saw red. I'm sorry. I didn't mean to hurt her."

Moore felt like they were on a roll. She had seen this previously when dealing with killers. Once they have been exposed, they sometimes couldn't stop talking. She decided to exploit the opportunity to the full.

"Tell us about Mrs Walker, Peter," Moore said.

"What do you want to know?"

"Well, how deeply is she involved in the activities that the girls get up to?"

"She's completely behind it. It's her gig. I found out what she was up to and begged her to stop it. It wasn't right. Those students are pretty innocent and easily led astray. But Walker said she had to keep it up. Apparently, the school is losing loads of money, and it was only the business at Ozone that was keeping things afloat. She even had Gabriella importing drugs for her too. I think she worked with Larry at Ozone to distribute them. Have you got her in here too?"

"No, she's helping one of our colleagues from another unit with enquiries, but what you have told us will be very useful to them. It sounds as if she may be prosecuted under sex trafficking legislation, as well as living off immoral earnings."

"Good enough for her. She's a bad egg."

Moore thought that this was a bit rich coming from a double murderer, but said nothing.

"While we are here, Peter, what do you know about damage to my car?" Moore said.

"Oh, I'm sorry about that. I just wanted to create a distraction to try and throw you off the scent. Did you get it fixed up?"

"Yes, but it cost almost €1,000, so I'll be looking for reimbursement for that too. And you scared the daylights out of me as well."

Ledwidge said nothing. He buried his head in his hands.

* * *

"What do you want us to do with Roberts, sir?" Burke was sitting with Superintendent Jerome Heffernan in his splendid office at the top of Store Street Garda station.

"Stupid fecker. What exactly have we got on him, Aidan?"

"Apart from a few motoring offences, not a lot. I don't think the DPP would buy conspiracy to murder. After all, he wasn't to know that Ledwidge intended to strangle the girl, was he? And he has been helpful to us, I suppose."

"But I thought you found his car close to the scene of one of the murders, or did I imagine that bit?" Heffernan said.

"We did, sir. But it seems that was just a coincidence. He told us he was driving up along the canal when the car just stopped. He couldn't get it started again, so he let it roll down the hill and it just happened to come to a halt where we found it. I know it sounds a bit off, but there's no evidence to contradict his story, none at all. Even a tissue we found in the footwell had none of the girl's DNA on it, and there were no further traces to say that she had been in the car," Burke said.

"You know what? I'm fed up with these Brits coming over here and thinking they can mix it up with us. I'd like to make an example of him, but I see what you're saying about the DPP. Tell you what, why don't you take him for a drive?"

"A drive, sir?"

"Yes, a nice long drive in a northerly direction. I'll make a phone call, and we can arrange to have him met. I hear Blacklion and Belcoo are good places for such an endeavour."

"God, that brings back memories. I remember when I was a kid, Mars bars and Spangles couldn't be had in Ireland due to protective regulations for our indigenous industries. My father used to have business up that way, and we'd drive to Blacklion and stop the car, walk across to Belcoo and fill a big bag with the illicit sweets. I was fierce popular in national school after those trips. Yes, boss, sounds like a great idea."

Epilogue

Peter Ledwidge was charged with two counts of murder and remanded on bail until his trial several months later. With the forensic evidence that the Gardaí had collected, and the testimony that he himself had provided, his guilt was not in doubt. He was given a life sentence in Mountjoy jail.

Darren Roberts went for a drive with Inspector Burke. At Blacklion, Roddy McClintock was waiting for him at the bridge that separated the two jurisdictions, and Roberts was duly handed over. He also spent some time in jail for the crimes he had committed in the United Kingdom. He vowed never to go back to Ireland as long as he lived. He had had enough of the place to last a lifetime.

The World of English is still going. Janet O'Sullivan took it over. She used the €15,000 she had loaned the place to purchase it outright. She quickly moved the operation to smaller premises nearer the city centre, and refocused recruitment on South East Asia, which she found to be a lucrative source of candidates very keen to come to Dublin to learn English. Under her management, the school was now very profitable, and the memories of what had been in the past quickly faded.

Edith Walker didn't fare so well. She was accused of trafficking for the purpose of sexual exploitation, pimping, and living off immoral earnings. The press went to town on her, and the trial that she faced the following year made headline news. She was sentenced to a total of ten years in jail, but with the last three suspended.

Ozone was shut down. Larry Fitzgerald was in fact the owner of the place, but it turned out that there were tax and licensing issues with it, and Revenue eventually seized Larry's home, car and worldly goods, although the man himself escaped incarceration.

Burke's little 'spot of bother' went away. The woman who was out to make trouble for him had relented and settled for the original sentence that had been handed down to her, and GSOC closed the file. No entry concerning the matter was logged in Burke's record, thanks to some deft manoeuvring by Superintendent Heffernan.

Maria Gomez turned up back in Spain. She recognised that she had had a close encounter in Dublin and vowed never to travel there again.

Burke, Moore, Lawler and Sutton were highly praised for their work on the case. O'Higgins recognised the very significant input they had made to his case against Edith Walker, and though there was talk of some formal recognition of their joint efforts, nothing came of it. Crime in Dublin didn't wait long to get their attention once again, and soon it was back to business as usual.

Character List

Detective Inspector Aidan Burke – a tough, and sometimes rough, member of An Garda Síochána with a rather barren love life.

Detective Sergeant Fiona Moore – a clever detective who works with Burke and sometimes outsmarts him.

Detective Garda Dónal Lawler – a diligent member of the detective team in Store Street Garda station.

Detective Garda Amy Sutton – a junior detective that shows a lot of promise.

Jerome Heffernan – a wily detective superintendent originally from Cork.

Aileen Brophy – the state pathologist.

Keith Malone & Ruth Maguire – forensic officers.

Michael Kelleher – a motorcycle Garda.

Edith Walker – principal of The World of English.

Janet O'Sullivan – Mrs Walker's loyal assistant.

Karla – receptionist at The World of English.

Larry – barman at Ozone, a rather seedy nightclub in Dublin.

Darren Roberts – a visitor to Dublin with a rocky past and a liking for cheap cars.

Peter Ledwidge – a teacher at The World of English and a student at Trinity College.

Gabriella Ortez, Alicia Navarro, Maria Gomez, Isabella Hernandez and Alena Sanchez – Spanish students attending The World of English.

If you enjoyed this book, please let others know by leaving a quick review on Amazon. Also, if you spot anything untoward in the paperback, get in touch. We strive for the best quality and appreciate reader feedback.

ALSO IN THIS SERIES

A DEADLY DIVIDEND - BOOK 1

A man killed in a desolate alley. A woman attacked in her home. Two detectives who must connect these events, and hunt down a killer who doesn't give a damn.

A FATAL LIAISON - BOOK 2

A man is found dead in his car in a forest outside of Dublin. Very dead. There is quite a mess. The police suspect foul play and call in the detectives. It is not long before another body is found in the area. A full-scale murder inquiry is launched. Can DI Aidan Burke and DS Fiona Moore collar the killer?

THE CHINA CHAPTER - BOOK 3

A man killed in a house fire. Badly burned, but shot before the flames are set. When discovered, the weapon points to a China connection, but are detectives just being led away from a motive far closer to home?

LETHAL IN SMALL DOSES - BOOK 4

The race is on to collar a killer who is targeting the elderly in care homes. If DS Fiona Moore can better understand his motive, she can track him down. But sidelined by her boss, might her eagerness to stop the murderer get her into danger?

PLANE DEAD - BOOK 5

A plane lands at Dublin airport with a dead passenger – poisoned, and for once not by the inflight menu. Detective Fiona Moore is sure he's been murdered, and investigates.

All FREE with Kindle Unlimited and available in paperback from Amazon.

OTHER BOOKS BY DAVID PEARSON

In the Galway Homicides series:

Murder on the Old Bog Road (Book 1)
Murder at the Old Cottage (Book 2)
Murder on the West Coast (Book 3)
Murder at the Pony Show (Book 4)
Murder on Pay Day (Book 5)
Murder in the Air (Book 6)
Murder at the Holiday Home (Book 7)
Murder on the Peninsula (Book 8)
Murder at the Races (Book 9)
Murder in a Safe Haven (Book 10)
Murder in an Irish Bog (Book 11)
Murder in a Seaside Town (Book 12)

Available in paperback and free with Kindle Unlimited

www.thebookfolks.com

Made in the USA
Monee, IL
27 April 2022

95553885R00142